A *heart* IN *port*

# A *heart* IN *port*

EMILY GIVNER

*thistledown press*

No part of this publication may be reproduced or transmitted in any form
or by any means, graphic, electronic or mechanical, including photocopying,
recording, or any information storage and retrieval system, without permission
in writing from the publisher or a licence from The Canadian Copyright
Licensing Agency (Accesss Copyright). For an Access Copyright licence, visit
www.accesscopyright.ca or call toll free to 1-800-893-5777.

Library and Archives Canada Cataloguing in Publication

Givner, Emily, 1966-2004.
A heart in port / Emily Givner.

Short stories.
ISBN 978-1-897235-32-4

I. Title.

PS8613.I86H43 2007        C813'.6        C2007-904529-4

Cover photograph© Elliot/zefa/Corbis
Cover and book design by Jackie Forrie
Printed and bound in Canada

Thistledown Press Ltd.
633 Main Street
Saskatoon, Saskatchewan, S7H 0J8
www.thistledownpress.com

 Canada Council   Conseil des Arts
for the Arts    du Canada

 Canadian    Patrimoine
Heritage     canadien

Thistledown Press gratefully acknowledges the financial assistance of the
Canada Council for the Arts, the Saskatchewan Arts Board, and the Government
of Canada through the Book Publishing Industry Development Program for
its publishing program.

"In-Sook" was first published in *Grain*, and "The Resemblance Between a Violin Case and a Cockroach" in *Wascana Review*. "Canadian Mint" appeared in *The Toronto Star* as a winner in the summer fiction competition

# CONTENTS

# PREFACE

THE TITLE STORY of this collection is a lighthearted gloss upon heartbreak, a jester's choreography of illness and disappointment. The title itself, for a story set in Halifax, is a play upon words and meanings — at once nod and counterpoint to Emily Dickinson's epigraph.

The whole book works in this way. To describe Emily Givner's work thematically could suggest a grimness that would wholly distort the actual delight in her writing, for I can think of very few writers in whose work gaiety and sadness are so inextricably linked.

None of her stories, in fact, has a single focus, though they move with so light a touch and with a story-teller's ease. Emily was never interested in Chekhov's much quoted *art of the glimpse* — the worlds she was intent on evoking in her stories were complex, immediate and alive with inherent contradictions. Origins and "back story" would not be sacrificed to sparse dramatic implication; random accidents would be allowed their relevance.

A ludicrous note in a Halifax shopkeeper's window forms both a relief from family claustrophobia and a segue to Asia and the bittersweet echoes of love. This is technically brilliant, but in a mode more common to novels. Many short story writers would see it as a "linear digression", irrelevant, undistilled. Emily saw that the short story today could essay what the novel once did. Her energy fed on the disparate.

She wrote to her mother, the writer Joan Givner, "I am not particularly comfortable with the pared down, classic short story form, as I don't see life that way. I very much identify with the chaotic form of Alice Munro's later stories." Her ambivalent fascination with Munro's "White Dump" is revealing. "I loved certain parts of the story," she wrote, "but, it really is overstuffed, which I appreciate also." And again: "The strength of that story is not diminished by its weird structure and so many bizarre inclusions. I think in all strong writing there is something very weird."

"Only when I was in the middle of writing a story," says Virginia in "Freedom Holes", "did I realize a certain thing had happened, that I had actually wanted it to happen, like an orphan who shows up on your doorstep and says. *You may not know me, my name is Rachel, but you have always known me and your name is Rachel too.*"

"Freedom Holes" may be closest in this collection to being a straightforward, single-strand story, but it contains both that aesthetic statement, and an insight into a writer in the making:

"If I had met Elmer in any other environment, I doubt I would have described myself as a writer. After all, I hadn't published a thing. I carried *Best American Short Stories* around like a bible in my rucksack and scribbled bits of dialogue in notebooks while drinking coffee in the cafés along Spring Garden Road, but that was about it."

This is not gratuitous autobiography (though no doubt it *is* a footnote to a stage in Emily's short life), because it reflects so well on the story itself, which is full of surprises: unexpected and joyous quirks of humanity behind every door that the hapless sales force knocks upon. Here is an author *listening*, as a writer friend expressed it to me, *not controlling* — as a writer *must* listen if her characters are to have their own lives, and the story its own integrity.

And those "scribbled bits of dialogue" hint at her marvellous ear for cadence and for the revealing, often comical, turns of phrase that enliven these stories. Language, both thought and spoken, is a playground for Emily Givner, a source of merriment but also of wistful consequence. One silly pun (PAINTING STUDIO defaced to PANTING STUD) leads to a life's dislocation; another (scheduling a disappointment with the doctor) will resonate with anyone who has lived, as Emily did, with a chronic ailment.

Her enjoyment of dialogue as its own style of storytelling, may reflect her time as a drama student (though the university scenes in "The Blue Lobster" are aglint with mockery). She makes a dramatist's demand that the audience *listen* too, and do some of the work. Speech does not always communicate; conversations must be unravelled:

"The back seat was filled with paint cans and brushes. "Those brushes are mine," Murray said, eyeing them. "You borrowed them a year ago, you should return them."

"Don't twist your head around. It might affect your neck," said Leda.

"Why?" Beth asked. "It's not as though you use them."("A Heart in Port")

or:

"What if the same people are outside?" she said. "What will they think, especially after everyone took pity on me?"

"How do you know they took pity on you?" the gentleman said.

"Don't worry, Gwen!" the prophet shouted from behind his curtain. "The world's gonna end anyway. On December the twelfth."

"Will you stop that nonsense!" the gentleman groaned, "I think we've had enough of that!"

"I could just tell," Gwen said. ("The Graveyard")

What the reader gets out of this demand, of course, is fun. And a vivid sense of being present in the story.

These stories are never quite what they present themselves as being. In some — like "Canadian Mint" and "Private Eye" — a small apparent flaw in the story's internal logic creates a puzzle and a hint, and to solve that puzzle the reader is led to go back to the story again and read it with new eyes. There is often something otherworldly afoot — too organic to be merely surreal, too witty to strain credibility.

When the glass eye starts speaking to Andrzej, in "In-Sook", the voice takes us unawares, as it does him. The speaker is not identified at once. Perhaps it is only his intuition? Besides, In-Sook's eye, or rather its absence, is a comical aide-memoire for the forgetful girl — nothing gothic or numinous there. Nevertheless, a glass eye *is* speaking, and its words both conceal and reveal the infatuations of Andrzej's students. It's funny, and witty, and sad, and believable.

So, too, is "The Resemblance Between a Violin Case and a Cockroach", a story which (quite apart from its quiet prefiguring of Emily's own death) is a juggling act of improbability, fictional breakdown, sly rhetoric, fairytale and literary allusion, all sustained by the luminous sensibility and perceptions of the young girl, Clarissa. It shouldn't work, but it does. And the ending is at once the gentlest and saddest of scenes and an enigmatic ambush upon the reader.

There are three Eastern European musicians, married older lovers, in this collection. What is interesting to me in this is not the common denominator, but the very different ways that these characters are seen. Emily is working out variations on a theme — a common enough mode for painters and musicians, but one curiously distrusted in writers. I hope that, if Emily had lived, she would not have discarded any of them for that reason — each is its own, poignant self, and the final version in the title story carries a sense of completion, of a haunting measure refined and laid to rest.

Emily read widely, passionately and with a developing sense of taste, judgement and craft. The last two years of her life were devoted to writing.

All serious writers must hope (against hope, perhaps) that they have breathed enough life into their work, have done something original enough and worthy of the ancestors, for it to endure beyond themselves. It is a sorrow (one I've tried to restrain in this introduction) that Emily's work is here now — alert, funny, tender, inventive — while she is not.

*A note on the editing process:*

*It's a delicate matter to presume on a dead person's work. Apart from selecting the stories to be included here (there are many others) I've made very few changes. I have added perhaps 15 words in all, none of them tendentious. I have rearranged passages, without altering them, in two stories where I felt the time frames were unnecessarily challenging. Making decisions like that of course involved conversations — imaginary if you will — in which I tried to make these shifts seem commonsensical. It was the same with deletions — I removed some repetitions that I felt were excessive, and this was a delicate issue too, since Emily took pleasure at times in the mischievous cadence of repetition itself. Three or four paragraphs were also cut — not for their weakness, but because the stories in question seemed to move very well without them.*

*Joan Givner has been wonderfully generous, supportive and insightful, while keeping a professional distance except when I needed advice.*

Emily Givner's life as a writer was unfinished (she would have said, had scarcely begun) and I have ended this collection with "The Graveyard", itself unfinished. At the wild heart of the graveyard's deceptive symmetry, a woman in a green coat is standing in front of a gravestone, waiting for something to unfold . . .

Seán Virgo, 2007

# In-Sook

EVERYTHING, OR NEARLY everything the Polish professor said, included the words, my wife. It didn't matter what they were doing — walking around the congested streets of Pusan, climbing a mountain, or sitting in air-conditioned coffee houses — the professor drinking espressos and smoking while In-Sook snacked on white bread slathered with white icing — my wife would not believe you Koreans eat this — the references piled up until In-Sook imagined the professor's wife gazing down on them from an elevated plane.

"My wife would never just sit in a coffee shop. She doesn't stop to rest. She wakes up at six in the morning, a bit gray from being too tired, makes sandwiches for our daughters to take to their schools for lunch and then she takes Kaja for a walk."

"Who's Kaja?" asked In-Sook. The professor had just pronounced the name of an ancient Korean kingdom.

"Our dog," said the professor. "I wanted to call my youngest daughter Kaja, but my wife said it wasn't a proper Christian name. Like most Poles, my wife is very Catholic, but more Catholic than most."

∽

In-Sook sat on the edge of the professor's bed. In one corner of the room, stood a coffee table covered with dust, a TV and a phone. She wondered if the professor watched Korean soap operas. The door to his walk-in closet was open, revealing a series of black tuxedos with long tails and peaked lapels, a red sports jacket, a pair of dress shoes and five empty bottles of juniper gin.

The professor picked up a lighter from the nightstand beside his bed and examined it. "It's a Cardin," he said, showing her the lighter. "It's a very good lighter, really it is. I received two more very good lighters as gifts."

Shortly after Director Park introduced him, the visiting professor was besieged by an army of gift-bearing students. Or at least that's the way In-Sook imagined he must have perceived it. They all arrived at his studio at once. There had been some debate as to whether they should approach him individually or as a group. In the end, they decided on all at once. It would take less of the professor's time and they tended to do things in groups anyway.

When he opened the door, they all cheered. He seemed surprised to see them all standing outside his door, blocking the hallway. "Come in, come in," he said.

With everyone packed inside, the studio seemed smaller, less airy than usual. In-Sook was familiar with the studio, the two grand pianos. The plaques on the door changed as the visiting professors came and went, but everything else remained the same.

Soon the professor's desk was awash with ribbon and stray paper. After he had opened several gifts, he placed them on the lid of the piano closest to the window. He wiped his forehead with the back of his hand and declared he needed a cigarette after all this opening which was hard work and he wanted to try out the beautiful lighter he had just received.

He smoked a cigarette, talked with his students, and then opened the next gift. It was another lighter engraved with his name, *Andrzej Sienkiewicz*

He received a traditional Korean theatre mask, a bottle of Ballantine's scotch whiskey of which he seemed terribly appreciative, a Korean calendar, a pocket watch, a bottle of plum wine, a polo shirt, a lacquered jewelry box the professor said would be a good place to keep his cufflinks. There were more things, but In-Sook couldn't remember them all.

In-Sook's friend, Soo-Young, had given the professor the polo shirt. For a week she had agonized over choosing the right size, appropriate colour and designer label. When Soo-Young had narrowed down her choices, she insisted In-Sook accompany her through the department stores to help make the final decision. Soo-Young finally settled on a shirt with dark green horizontal stripes. It would match the mossy green trousers the professor had sported on several occasions. He looked good in those trousers, they both agreed. They had not expected him to be so young and handsome. He was replacing the professor from Romania who was close to sixty and had problems walking. Acknowledging they weren't good at guessing the ages of foreigners, In-Sook and Soo-Young estimated the professor to be anywhere from thirty-eight to forty-three.

In-Sook had purchased a book with blank pages. She filled it with photos — her mother cooking rice for breakfast, the persimmon tree in the backyard, her sister in a Korean Airlines uniform. She labeled all the pictures, explaining that the building on the second last page was City Hall where her father worked as chief of the investment sector. The professor said later that he especially liked her gift because it had shown the most thought and care. In-Sook shook her head. She told him it simply wasn't true. He would never know how much thought Soo-Young had put into that polo shirt.

A fan by the window whirred, sending shreds of cigarette smoke around the room. "I don't know what I'll do with all these lighters," he said. "Maybe I'll give one to my wife. She doesn't smoke, but she can use it to light candles on All Saints Day. It's a very special holiday in Poland. She's so busy on All Saints Day — lighting candles, arranging flowers. My wife is perfect, really she is."

The professor paused to scratch his arm. "Are you Buddhist?" he asked.

In-Sook shook her head.

"You're Christian?" His eyes widened. They were blue, but not bright blue like a swimming pool. Blue, like the sky beginning to rinse itself with dusk. "No," In-Sook replied. "I'm nothing."

The professor cocked his head. He looked sympathetic. "Sometimes I wonder too. Even though in Poland, I go to the Holy Cross Church where Chopin's heart is buried in a pillar. You know about this heart, don't you?"

"No," she said.

"Chopin died when he was thirty-nine. He was living in France. Although he was buried in Paris, he made a special request that his heart be taken back to Poland. His sister carried it all the way in a bottle under her coat."

He sighed. "Unfortunately, because of this heart, the church has become a tourist attraction. Tourists, mostly Asians, come with their cameras and take photographs while people are praying. I know you Asians like taking photographs everywhere you go, but a church is not the place."

The professor said the last phrase with great authority. *A church is not the place.*

In-Sook felt ashamed on behalf of all Asians.

"Anyway, I thank you for bringing me this net. The mosquitoes were eating me alive like wolves."

∾

After her lesson devoted to Rachmaninov's *Rhapsody on a Theme by Paganini,* the professor knelt down to pull something out of his briefcase.

"It's a pity," he said, showing her an alarm clock. "It's a very good clock. I bought it in Poland, but now it is broken."

He seemed deeply upset by the fate of his clock. He looked exhausted and the skin on his left cheek was rough and dry. For the last month he hadn't been happy. Maybe he missed his family or wasn't eating right. He'd mentioned he didn't like Korean food, found it too hot and spicy. He should be sleeping better, protected by the mosquito net she'd attached to the ceiling above his bed. And Director Park had installed an air conditioner in his flat.

The whites of his eyes were turning yellow. She hoped he hadn't contracted hepatitis.

To cheer him up, In-Sook had brought him a strawberry smoothie from a new place by the school, not far from where she stepped off the bus. It sat on his desk, probably warm by now. While waiting in line, she had admired the exotic cakes displayed on shelves behind a thick layer of glass. Desserts laden with cream and fruit, lacy triangles of chocolate jutting from the tops, on an angle, like beautiful hair combs.

Things in her country were changing at a rapid rate. Italian coffee shops with European cakes, Korean girls wearing chopsticks in their hair, and now smoothies which a week ago she never knew existed. Behind the counter, machines that mixed drinks whirred furiously while workers zigzagged around, preparing sandwiches.

The professor had regarded the smoothie, warily. "Is there milk in it?"

"I don't know."

"I'm very allergic to milk. Years ago, I came in fourteenth in the second round of the Tchaikovsky competition. The morning before the final round, I ordered scrambled eggs in the hotel where I was staying."

"What's scrambled eggs?" She wondered if the professor might enjoy quails eggs, a traditional Korean side dish.

"Mmmm," said the professor, rubbing his chin, "eggs that have been broken, put into a pan, stirred around and fried. Anyway, to get back to my story, the cook put milk into my eggs and that afternoon, I was so shaky I couldn't play because allergies affect the muscles. I placed fourteenth," he said sadly. "If I hadn't eaten those eggs, my life would be a lot different. I probably wouldn't be here. I'd be traveling all over the world, making a lot of money, giving more concerts than I do."

In-Sook pondered the connection — if the cook hadn't put the milk in the scrambled eggs, then the professor wouldn't be in Korea. In a strange way she was glad the cook had added the milk, otherwise she would never have met him. But, she knew that was selfish.

"I know of a repair shop," she said. "Tomorrow, I will take the clock and see what can be done. I can't do it today, I have a party to go to."

"What kind of party?"

"A friend of mine just got married. It's a party where we ask the bride questions about married life."

"Oh," said the professor. "How long do you think it will take the repair shop to fix my clock?"

"I don't know."

"Meanwhile, I will need a new clock. That much is obvious. Would you take me shopping for one, when it's convenient?"

"Yes, it would be my pleasure."

It *was* her pleasure, and also a great honor serving as the professor's guide and assistant. Director Park had assured her she was the best candidate because, number one, she was pleasant to look at, number two, she was usually on campus, practising, and, number three, unlike the rest of the students, she spoke excellent English.

The task also involved a lot of responsibility, as Director Park made clear. "Show the professor where to buy food, take him to the Dong-A department store and the open markets. He'll want to see the temples. Inform him you'll clean his studio. Bring tea whenever he rings for it. And anything else you can think of."

The professor's jaw had dropped. "Clean my studio? You're a student, not a maid. I can clean my studio myself."

In-Sook had been horrified. "Please allow me to clean your studio. If Director Park spots dust, he'll be very angry with me." The moment she said it, she regretted it. She should have expressed a desire to dust, rather than involve Director Park.

In the end, the professor didn't mind. There was no shortage of work because he left his window open. He was amazed by the dust, wondered where it all came from.

She tried to explain. Industrial pollution, yellow winds blowing eastward from the Gobi desert in China. Smoke, at the moment, from several large fires on the Korean Peninsula.

The professor said he didn't want students to choke on his cigarette smoke. But he didn't know anymore. Perhaps he was letting more bad air in by not closing the window. And there wasn't time to walk down the three flights of stairs and outside, between lessons.

Cleaning his studio made her happy. A damp cloth in her hand, she dusted the pianos, the bookshelf, the spokes of the electric fan. Thinking all the while that some day she'd make a good wife. Not a perfect wife like the professor's, but a good wife nonetheless.

The professor's face clouded over. "How will I wake up tomorrow without my clock?"

"I'll call you."

"Seven o'clock. Are you sure you'll remember?"

"Hopefully."

"In-Sook, you have a terrible memory for everything except music, you even said so. If you don't write things down, you forget."

She nodded, and the worst thing was, she often forgot where she wrote things. Her poor memory was a liability, something she'd tried to hide from all the boys she'd ever dated.

If one of them decided to marry her, he'd worry she'd tell their children to wait over there by the woman selling sesame leaves and then forget where they were. "You won't forget," her mother had assured her on numerous occasions, "that kind of memory comes with childbearing."

In-Sook thought of something. She reached for her purse and pulled out an eye patch made of black silk. Turning her back, she removed her right eye and put on the patch. Then faced him.

"Now, I know I'll remember to call you. Please keep this for me," she said and handed him the glass eyeball. "If you don't, I'll put it some place and there's good chance I'll forget where."

"I — I don't understand," said the professor.

"When I wake up tomorrow morning, I'll look in the mirror to wash my face and brush my hair. When I see my eye is gone, I'll remember to call you."

"Will you remember *why* your eye is missing?" He looked worried.

"I'll remember."

"Sometimes in Poland, we tie a string around our finger if we don't want to forget something."

"I can't do that. People will think it's cheap jewelry."

∾

Moon-Joo and her husband lived in a modest flat — a small living room, a tiny slice of kitchen with no stove but four burners. The flat was located on the fourth floor of the complex, providing a good view of the mountain range. Moon-Joo was lucky to have a flat so high up. The flats on the first and second floors overlooked the parking lot in front of the building and the busy highway beyond.

Above a cabinet inlaid with mother-of-pearl, there was a picture of Moon Joo in her wedding dress, a photo so doctored up, it could appear in a magazine.

Most of the guests had arrived, girls from the neighborhood and university. They brought plates of food their mothers had made. Fried squid, rice noodles in hot sauce sprinkled with sesame seeds, kimchi pancakes.

A week earlier, In-Sook had taken her English Conversation teacher, Andrew from Canada, for dinner at Pizza Hut. The large pizza had just arrived when her cell phone rang, an electronic rendition *of Für Elise.* "It's my mother," she said to Andrew, "one minute."

Four pieces of pizza sat on the platter, but In-Sook knew she had to leave, to make some kind of excuse. "You come home right now!" her mother had screamed over the phone. "I don't want you spending time with foreigners!"

Her mother was probably worried she'd marry a foreigner, like the daughter of one of the neighbors. That she'd have a son-in-law with whom she couldn't communicate, who didn't understand The Korean Way.

It seemed all the male foreigners who came to Korea ended up taking Korean wives. Her mother considered them — mostly English teachers or members of the American military — a form of pollution linked to fast food restaurants and movies filled with sex and violence.

But Andrzej Sienkiewicz was another story. Her mother didn't view him as a pollutant because he was a respectable person, a concert pianist who'd been invited to teach in Korea.

Her father took a special interest in the professor, even bought a book about the history of Poland. While her mother watched TV, he sat beside her on a cushion on the floor reading it. He would shake his head and say, "The Poles are just like us, big countries coming at them from all sides."

Her father, in general, was open to foreigners. He had traveled to America several times on business, and twice a week, after work, attended an English class on the seventh floor of City Hall. It was mandatory, taught by an American woman in her thirties, whom her father said was very nice and polite.

"In her thirties? Why isn't she at home with her husband?" In-Sook's mother asked suspiciously.

Her father looked bruised. "She isn't married. It's very sad."

"The professor's married," said In-Sook.

"*Of course* he's married," said her mother.

Now, Moon-Joo was married. The girls sat around a low table in the living room, eager to hear what she had to say. They picked up peanuts and raw garlic from side plates and popped them in their mouths.

Moon-Joo explained she hadn't liked her husband very much before the wedding, but her parents wanted her to marry very badly. And it was the right time. Then, after the wedding, things changed. She liked her husband a lot, believed she even loved him.

In-Sook knew why. It was a powerful force that changed everything. She couldn't wait to get married and experience it. Although it was becoming more and more common, sex before marriage.

"Is it true," asked one of the girls, "that married couples have sex like dogs?" Several of the guests giggled. One cried out with disgust.

Moon Joo smiled. "Yes, it's true, and I know it sounds awful, but it isn't really. You'll understand when you're married."

"And is it true," asked the girl who cried out, "that he puts his tongue in your mouth and rolls it around like an earthworm?"

"Yes," said Moon Joo, "that is also true. When you're married, you'll understand. It won't seem strange at all."

∾

He gazed at the net hanging above his bed. It reminded him of the veil his wife had worn at their wedding. He poured two more fingers of gin and thought about the honeymoon all those years ago at the Baltic seaside. His wife had come down with a yeast infection and it had rained the entire time. They both agreed they should have stayed home. They could have feasted on what was left of the wedding food.

Tonight he had called her, as he did every second day. She said his mother-in-law who lived with them had blood in her urine and the vacuum cleaner wasn't working. It would cost five hundred zlotys to fix it and she wasn't sure if there was any point in having the Ukrainian housekeeper come in.

He could picture the Rainbow vacuum cleaner he'd paid a fortune for sitting in a musty workshop somewhere in Warsaw and felt quite sorry for it. He told his wife something had happened to his alarm o'clock and In-Sook would take him shopping for a new one as soon as possible.

"You should be more independent," his wife scolded. "You should go out alone and buy one. Why does she have to accompany you?"

He tried to explain that it wasn't easy buying things in a foreign country. He wanted to ask questions about the alarm o'clock, its warranty, and he only knew a few words of Korean.

The conversation had ended abruptly after that.

He wanted to tell his wife about the glass eye, but after the tone she used with him, he decided against it.

In-Sook's eye was on the table in front of him, beside his bottle of jumper gin. All day he'd walked around with it in the bottom of his jacket pocket. It had stared at him while he talked to his wife. He thought of Chopin's sister carrying that bottle under her coat all the way back to Poland. What a dangerous journey it must have been, crossing all those borders.

Had the story he told In-Sook about Chopin's heart inspired her to give him the eye? He doubted it. But what a strange thing for her to do. There was something unusual about her, the way she interpreted certain pieces of music. It's what made her such a good pianist, besides the fact that she practised all the time. As he'd told Soo-Young, talent was not just something you're born with. The desire to do something, take risks, make sacrifices were all branches of talent. Talent meant nothing unless you had the courage to live up to it.

Soo-Young had agreed. In general, she was having problems playing. He'd noticed on certain days her hands trembled and he suspected she was allergic to milk. He'd read somewhere that many Asians were. A few days ago, he'd suggested she cut milk out of her diet.

He poured himself two more fingers of gin. He picked up the eyeball and rolled it around in his palm. "I think she's allergic to milk. What do you think?" he said to the eye.

He put it in his mouth. It tasted of nothing special, like a marble. He wished he had someone to talk to. He felt so lonely. But he often felt lonely, even in the presence of his family. He loved his wife, but her entire existence revolved around duty. She was constantly moving, getting this done, that done, whereas he needed time to think. To sit in a chair mulling things over. Which she interpreted as laziness.

Or maybe it wasn't thinking he needed time for, but feeling. To sit and feel. Try and figure out a passage he was working on, how to feel it in order to play it properly.

He took the eyeball out of his mouth and set it on the table. "What if I'd swallowed you?" he asked. "Wouldn't that be a disaster? How would I explain that to In-Sook?" He wondered where the eye would go. If it would land in his appendix or if he'd find it in the toilet.

"Soo-Young trembles because she's in love with you. She can't concentrate when you're watching her."

"Really?"

"Yes," said the eye.

"She's very beautiful," he said, smiling.

"No, she's not."

"She has high cheekbones and those big brown eyes."

"Yes, she has high cheekbones, a square jaw and dark skin. I am a traditional Korean beauty with a face like a moon, placid as a lake."

"She has big breasts."

The eye didn't say anything.

"You should be green," he said. He had always loved green eyes. "Yes, you should be green, the colour of youth and jealousy."

"And our mountains," the eye added. "Last weekend when I went mountain climbing, I thought of your shoulders, the way they slope down gently."

"I wonder what you'd be like in bed. I've thought about Soo-Young, never you. But, now we've had this conversation . . . "

He took the eye and moved it to his bedside table where his alarm clock should be. He'd had too much to drink as usual and was ready for sleep. After flicking off the overhead light, he pulled back the mosquito net and crawled in between the sheets. He hadn't brushed his teeth and his tongue tasted sour. He turned over in bed and stared at the eye, what he could see of it.

∾

The next day, In-Sook and Soo-Young sat on a park bench by the crepe myrtle tree. Soo-Young was desperate. Her eyes were as red as the tree's flowers. She'd been to the beauty salon and got a bad permanent. Her long hair looked zapped by an electrical force, and In-Sook didn't know how to soothe her.

Soo-Young started crying again. A small Winnie-the-Pooh doll attached to the strap of her shoulder bag grinned, the bear's red shirt riding high above its fat stomach. "He won't think I'm pretty anymore," said Soo-Young.

Did Soo Young's boyfriend really think she was pretty? Objectively she wasn't. Soo-Young must have been worried that her boyfriend, once he laid eyes on her frazzled hair, would leave her. But Soo-Young's boyfriend would leave anyway. He had to go away for years of compulsory military training and few relationships survived that.

"I'm sure he'll still think you're pretty. Besides, he's going away soon. When he leaves, give him a photograph of yourself with your old hair so that's the way he'll remember you. And by the time he comes back, your permanent will have grown out."

"I'm not talking about my boyfriend," said Soo-Young softly. "I'm talking about the professor. I think I love him. He cares so much about me. He advised me to stop drinking milk."

"I know," said In-Sook.

"How do you know?"

In-Sook wasn't sure. Last night, after brushing her teeth and removing her eye patch, she had a dream. The professor was making love to Soo-Young. He was lying beside her, his face between her breasts. Eventually, he put himself inside her. Soo-Young cried out, but her cry became the cry of In-Sook's mother. "What are you doing?" her mother screamed.

In-Sook woke up, full of fear, then fell back asleep. She had another dream. Above her, a nest of chest hair. He wore a golden cross around his neck. She'd never seen it before, as he kept it hidden beneath his shirts. It dangled, swayed slightly, over her face. He changed position, putting his weight on his elbows, closing the gap between their bodies. She opened her mouth and the cross fell in. On her tongue. Then partway down her throat.

∾

"It is considered one of the big tragedies in Korea, to meet your destiny too early or too late."

"Did we meet too early or too late?" asked the professor, stroking her belly.

"I'm not sure," said In-Sook. "Often, time is a stream that flows in both directions."

The first time he touched her, she experienced the profoundest form of forgetting yet. She neglected to consider Soo-Young, but much worse, she forgot about the professor's wife and children. He hadn't mentioned his wife in quite a while. "What if you wife knew about us?"

"She would want to kill me."

"Would she ask for a divorce?"

"Oh no, she's much too Catholic for that."

"Did you buy that necklace?" asked In-Sook, touching the cross with her finger.

"No, my wife did," he said, looking down at it. "Last year, for my fortieth birthday. A composer once told me forty is a very hard border to cross, and he was right. On my birthday, I went out with this composer and came home drunk. My wife said she had a gift, but wouldn't give it to me because I'd been rude to her. The next day I waited for my gift but it never came. She kept the gift for two weeks. When she finally gave it to me, it wasn't like a gift at all. I felt terrible."

"I understand," said In-Sook. "Some things in life are hard to bear."

# Canadian Mint

It was my idea, Eddie basically just hangs out. He separates the pennies from the loonies, the loonies from the toonies, the bills he stuffs in his pocket. Every time someone throws me a bill, he looks totally stunned, like we won the lottery, partied it away in a week and won it all over again the following Saturday.

It's the middle of summer, he's wearing a lumberjack shirt, but at least he's company. I'm building a tower out of pennies. Right now, it's three feet tall. It was my idea, but Eddie supplied the pennies. Couple of days ago, we were over at his place, this room with a mattress, a Nirvana poster taped to the wall and no TV. Man, I was bored. "Eddie," I said, "got any money?"

"Huh?" Eddie's like that, it usually takes him a couple of times.

"Money, man, got any money?"

He got up off the mattress and walked to the closet. He disappeared for a moment behind the white door and came back with a huge tobacco can. Export A Mild. It rattled with coins. My heart started pounding in my chest cause I could've really used a meatball sub, a large Coke and a couple of games of pool. It took him like ten blasted minutes to get the can open. I just sat there, tapping my foot, my stomach doing cartwheels. When he finally got it open, there was nothing but pennies. I poured the whole can out on the mattress, looking for a loonie, quarters, anything. Nothing but pennies. Mind you, there must've been three thousand pennies.

I thought of rolling the pennies. I'd done it before once, on Halloween. I had tape, paper, a bunch of pennies and a pen. "Dimes," I wrote, and took the roll down to the 7-Eleven.

The place was hopping, ghosts up and down the aisles. I slammed my roll down on the counter. "Nice costume," I said to the cashier. Meaning the tie, nametag and tight polyester pants. She looked at me suspiciously from under her crimson visor. "Dimes, you say? Five dollars worth of dimes?"

"That's right."

She cracked the roll open, right then and there, on the side of the counter. One of the sickest sounds I've ever heard, like someone falling down the basement stairs and smashing their head on an empty aquarium, which Eddie will tell you happened to his brother.

"Nice try, kid." She made me stand there while she counted the pennies. "Thirty-two pennies," she announced like I made her do the dishes. "Fifty pennies make up a roll. I can't even give you two quarters." She shoved the pennies to one side and sprayed the area where the pennies had been sitting with a bottle of blue cleaning fluid. After that was done, she put her hands on her hips, and said, "You have enough for sixteen Double Bubble bubble gums or sixteen Black Cat bubble gums, whichever you prefer. They're in the second aisle to your right, third shelf down."

"That's OK. I think I'll keep my pennies."

If there's one thing I learned from the whole experience, it's that fifty pennies make up a roll. Three thousand pennies, sixty rolls. First of all, I needed paper. "Eddie," I said, "got any paper?"

"Paper?" He reached into his pants pocket and pulled out some rolling papers, ZigZag blue. "No, Eddie, I mean sheets of paper, loose-leaf, foolscap. I want to roll some of these here pennies."

"No man," Eddie said, "no paper."

"You mean you don't got one single piece of paper in this entire room?"

"Nope," said Eddie, "no paper."

"Drag!" I shouted and started pacing around the room.

"I know," Eddie shouted back, trying to share in my outrage. "Drag, man."

The fact was, the pennies were useless. Now, I don't know if you know this or not, but you can't take a can full of pennies, and plunk them down in a Subway or Seven-Eleven. They want them rolled. They'll take up to forty-nine pennies unrolled, but fifty pennies or over, they'll say, "Roll them," or, "Go home and roll them," or, "Go home and bring them back rolled," depending what mood they're in.

I took Eddie's pillow, put it under my bum and sat on the floor.

"Christ," said Eddie, "I sleep on that."

"Sorry, man." I threw the pillow back on the bed.

"You know Eddie, whoever makes pennies, should stop making them. They're not worth the copper they're made of.

They're worth nothing. I bet rich people don't even deal with them."

"They don't deal with money period," Eddie said. "They use plastic, credit cards."

Honest to God, I was totally shocked. For Eddie, this was a major insight. I'd never heard him make an insight before and he sure as hell hasn't made one since. In any case, it must've taken a lot out of him, cause he looked tired. He lay back on the mattress and shut his eyes. It was two in the morning and I didn't feel like leaving. To tell you the truth, I just wanted to lie down beside him and fall asleep. It seemed weird though, so I decided against it.

I swooped the pennies off the mattress and started playing with them. I thought about what Eddie had said about credit cards, the rich people I saw everyday on their way to work. I thought about office buildings and my life on the streets. I thought about nothing, how every form of life in the entire universe comes from nothing or an atom that was always there, just hanging out. Before I knew it, I'd built this tower out of pennies. It's amazing what you can get done when you have a bit of quiet time.

I can't remember who woke up first. It could've been Eddie, but it could've been me. I remember looking for some extra blankets and then falling asleep with my head on Eddie's lumberjack shirt. "Wow," Eddie said, when he saw my penny building, *"ever awesome."* He stumbled out of the room. Halfway down the hall, he stopped and I could hear him peeing — the sound of a garden hose shutting on and off. When he came back, his eyes were glassy, like he'd smoked a reefer. He pointed to my tower of pennies. "Know what? I think we should take that act to the street."

"The street? What the hell are you talking about?"

"The street. Build it again on the street. We'll make a sign asking people for their pennies to make it bigger. As you said last night, no one wants them anyway."

"Then we'll roll the pennies," I screamed. "By then we'll have five thousand pennies."

"Damn right. Deal?"

"Deal," I said. And we both shook hands.

That afternoon we were all set up. Eddie had found a cardboard box in a storeroom. A pen. We tore a flap off and printed in big letters, HELP US OUT WITH A PENNY. PLEASE AND THANK-YOU. Then we hit the streets.

First thing, Eddie and I got in an argument. We found a good street, real busy, but there was a clown walking around on stilts, about three street bums begging for money, and a lady in a nice pink dress playing the accordion.

"No way, man," I said. "*Way* too much competition."

"Screw the competition," Eddie said.

"No way, man."

He turned around and grabbed my shoulders. "You know what your problem is? Low self-esteem."

"Where the hell d'ya get that line? Your social worker?" He released me, and now I think back to it, he looked kind of guilty.

A couple of seconds passed and he gave me a shove. "Alright, buddy," he said. "All I'm saying is, it's not everyone on God's green earth who can make a tower out of pennies."

"*Jeez*, Eddie! God's green earth? Where d'ya come up with this shit?"

I was getting pretty worked up, so I sat down on a curb to chill. I put my head in my hands and thought hard. This was the street, I decided. If I didn't set up here, Eddie would think I couldn't handle the competition. He'd call me a wimp, or say I had low self-esteem, and I just couldn't handle that.

Finally, I hauled myself up. "All right, Ed."

We sat down across from some office building, and I set to work. The first day went OK, I guess. Eddie and I started to notice a strange pattern. People, when they noticed our tower, stopped and smiled. They fumbled around for their pennies, threw in a dime or a quarter, sometimes more. It got to the point where Eddie, who was doing nothing but watching them — and collecting their money — could tell exactly what they were thinking. He gave me a running commentary. "That's right, buddy, cough it up, it's only a penny, ahhhh, what do you know, you gotta buncha pennies, more trouble than they're worth, eh? *Hell with it*, give the poor kids a quarter. Why not a loonie?"

Six-thirty, we packed everything up. The clown on stilts came over. He said he'd had a really shitty day so we offered to treat him at the Burger King down the block. From what Eddie figured, we had about fifteen dollars worth of silver, plus thousands of pennies. The clown gave us a traveling case to put our pennies in, on condition we returned it when we found something better. "Not a bad head," said Eddie later that night. He rambled on, but this time I fell asleep first.

The next morning, we started early. We'd decided the night before not to roll the pennies, to keep them as building material for the tower. By noon, it was three feet tall.

I was so hung up on my work, I didn't realize four hours had passed until Eddie said, "I think it's the lunch crowd." The street sounds, I blocked right out — shoes slapping the pavement, traffic, even Eddie's ongoing commentaries. He basically just sat there, reading people's minds or humming some old Nirvana tune. Every once in a while, he'd sort out the change. Actually, Eddie had gotten smart. Instead of running around collecting change off the pavement, he just held out his greasy baseball cap, like a basketball hoop, so passers-by would aim straight for the net.

As I was laying down more foundation to make the tower wider, Eddie and I had our second scrap. He'd bought a bag of sunflower seeds and the shells, wet and sticky, were scattered everywhere.

"Ed," I said. "I don't mind you yakking away or humming tunes, but I need a clean work area. I can't take these wet little sticky things shooting past me like missiles."

"Sorry man." He started piling them up, continued cracking and spitting, this time into his hand. I ignored him and went on widening my tower. When I looked up, like forty minutes later, he was trying to build a tower out of the shells. And, it wasn't a tower, anyway, it was this big soggy pile.

I freaked right out, and kicked down my tower.

Eddie said, real quiet, real slow-like, "*What* is your problem?"

Man, I was mad. Instead of trying to work things out, I took off, leaving Eddie with everything — the pennies, the sign, the silver.

Turns out, the clown helped him carry the stuff home. Then they went out for drinks and showed up about ten o'clock at my place, completely plastered. The clown said he paid for everything, but I somehow doubt it. Anyway, they brought me a bottle of vodka. After a couple of drinks, we decided it was nobody's fault. The clown said what Eddie was doing with the sunflower seeds, "ruined the effect" of the tower. Not only that, Eddie said if I'd told him the pile was bothering him, he would have put the seeds in a brown paper bag. The clown interrupted, telling me I'd flown off the handle.

"What handle?"

"If you two are planning to be business partners," he said, "you'd better learn to get along. Trust me," he said, "I'm talking from personal experience."

"That's a good one," I snorted. "Like what? Some clown partnership?"

Then Eddie lost it. He started rolling around the floor screaming with laughter. "Some clown partnership! Man, that's good, *some clown partnership.*"

Then I lost it, and we were both rolling around together.

"Well," the clown said finally, "I think I'll get going."

The next morning, of course, Eddie had a major hangover. He did nothing but sit there. He couldn't even be bothered to hold out his baseball cap. It just lay there on the sidewalk.

"I think it's about time you dummied up," I told him.

"You know what?" he groaned. "I need some time off. Like a spare or something, I remember in grade nine, I had this spare. Between English and Gym."

"Oh yeah? And what did you do?"

"Aw, nothing. Sat in the parking lot, had a smoke."

I was about to say, Eddie, your whole life has been a spare, but right then a suit stopped and threw us a five. He wouldn't leave. He kept standing there, staring. To be honest, he scared me. Great, I thought, just what we need. With my luck, he'll kick down my tower. He might even shoot me. I considered calling the clown over. Eddie, of course, was too hung over to think about anything.

Then the suit introduced himself. "I'm Malcolm Hoffman, and I'm a performance artist."

"Come again?" said Eddie. (Like I told you, it usually takes him a couple of times.)

The performance artist smiled. "A performance artist from New York." He rubbed his chin for a while. "This is the best piece of performance art I've seen in years. It's absolutely stunning." He yakked on for a while. "It addresses so many issues — poverty, the structure of capitalism. And, yes, public art, the art gallery as a kind of prison, or should I say, aesthetic fishbowl."

I felt bad for Eddie. The word 'fishbowl' must've reminded him of his brother lying at the bottom of the basement steps, bleeding to death by that stupid aquarium, dying slowly.

"I'll return tomorrow," the artist announced, "'with a video camera and perhaps a few of my friends. Will you be here?" He looked kind of worried.

But, I never really left, have lived inside the shelter of my brother's head for eleven years. Talking up a storm, or just passing through him, a steady stream of thought.

"I'll be here," said Eddie. "Sure as that lineup in front of the Burger King. Now it has that two-for-one deal."

# Private Eye

IT CAME DOWN to a geometry test, some kind of triangle I couldn't figure out. At the time I remembered a Triangle, one of the world's mysteries where planes got sucked out of the sky. Up till then, I had perfect marks in the class, in pretty well every class except phys-ed. I wasn't that great at sports involving a ball, but track and field was another story. Although I was small, I had a short torso and these daddy long legs. Running came naturally which might explain everything.

After the triangle, my life took a sharp turn. I dropped out of high school, suddenly, like Smarties from a candy machine. I took all the money I made working at the roller skating rink out of the bank. The next thing was a bus ticket to somewhere that wasn't Saskatchewan. I was sick of living squished in between Manitoba and Alberta. On the bus, it seemed I was sailing across a buttermilk pancake. My father used to say the prairies were a great psychic space, but out on the highway, I could have sworn I was Didi.

Weekends, Didi would do crazy eights around the roller rink. Then sometimes she'd just collapse, her whole body rolling in different directions. "It's something to do with my brain," she once explained. "I can't handle the flashes." I looked up at the balls of crushed mirror hanging from the ceiling. They sent slivers, the colours of the northern lights, everywhere. Psychic space my ass, I thought as the wheat waved goodbye.

My bus ticket said Calgary, although why I wasn't sure. I must have chosen it, I guessed. Calgary is where the mountains first show themselves so high the snow never melts. When I got off the bus they appeared like my hipbones when I wasn't eating. I sat down in the bus depot with a cup of coffee to wonder what was next. An unshaven man sitting across from me kept winking. His t-shirt said, "If you love something, set it free, if it comes back to you, hunt it down and kill it." I hoped my father didn't try and hunt me down. He would follow dark and thick like maple syrup. This was killing him, I knew it.

I asked around for the cheapest hotel and finally found it, some no-name brand, but shelter all the same. Sure, I was still on the prairies, but here I was teetering on the edge. The horizon was an electrocardiograph, and on a clear day the mountains traced a heartbeat across the sky. In the following days, I left my hotel room only to buy bags of Cheddar-flavoured popcorn and bottles of Evian. It reassured me somehow to think that even though I was still on the prairies, the water of the French Alps was surging through my system.

"How much of your weight is made up of water?" I asked my friend from back home over the phone.

"Cameo, where the hell are you?" Glenda said.

"I called to find out how much of a person's weight is made up of water," I said.

"Well, think about it," Glenda said grimly. "When you're incinerated, your ashes fit into a coffee cup."

"Oh," I said.

"If your dad gets hold of you, you'll know all about it. Where the hell are you anyway?"

"I'm taking a trip," I said.

"You're tripping out is what you're doing," said Glenda.

"I'm drinking a litre of Evian every day."

"So what?"

"I'm flushing out my system," I said.

"Cameo," Glenda said, "your body's not a toilet."

I started to wonder if my body wasn't a toilet after all. The rings around the toilet bowl were beginning to rival those around my eyes. At three in the morning, bikers would leave the bar downstairs, their Harleys sounding like lions with bronchitis.

"What right do they have, kickstarting the whole hotel into consciousness?" I asked the TV set.

The hardest thing was having no one to say good night to, no one except the anchorman on the late night news. No night was a good night anyway. I slept in past all possibility of maid service, waking up to the afternoon talk-shows. One thing about the talk-shows, they taught me things could actually be worse. The guests on *Oprah* have the worst problems imaginable. At first I thought the guests were actors. Then I realized this couldn't be true. It would be far easier to find people plagued with problems than actors who could capture those desperate personas so easily. Sometimes I would doze off and hear my parents wailing like lost children. But it was only the guests on a talk-show, their screams the soundtrack to my dreams.

When I told my parents 1 was dropping out, they turned vermillion red and said, "Well then, the world's your classroom." But the whole world slowly became the bar, dark and dank, full of men with forked tongues hiding from their wives.

"Baby, plug the table and we'll play," they'd say. So I started shooting pool and smoking cigarettes. Soon I became a pool shark, breaking triangles so the balls hit the banks and sank into pockets. Eightball after eightball, I played long after the last call. Even then, the men would prod me on, saying, "Come on baby, the graveyard's the place to rest."

One evening I called my parents so they didn't do something idiotic like call Missing Children or that TV show, *Unsolved Mysteries*. "You can't run away from yourself," my father said, his voice deep and earnest. I became overwhelmed with guilt, strong as a winter blizzard. If my father had fondled or bruised me, 1 could understand why I had bottomed out. As it was, I couldn't find a valid reason. I began to stutter like my straight A report cards. "See a counselor," my mother pleaded.

I decided a counselor might not be a bad idea. Anxiety and a poor diet had shredded my stomach lining, so I was drinking Malox along with rye and diet cokes. Eventually, I found a counselor called Donna.

"And what's your name?" Donna asked, as though I was slow in the head.

"Cameo, as in the brooch."

"Oh," said Donna, "I see." She used phrases like "straightening out" and "getting back on track."

What Donna didn't understand was I was now living for the rush. It didn't matter how I got it, as long as I got it. The lackluster structures of everyday life were as appealing as planal geometry or a prairie landscape. These were the starting blocks from which I sprinted.

Then suddenly, guess what? I ran into another runaway. He was leaning against the bar drinking tequila, looking strangely familiar. I filed through my mind, trying to give a name, an aftershave to the face. If he had been inside me, I'd probably have remembered. I mean, the guy beside him, some kind of director, I remembered undressing for sure. A Hawaiian shirt with palm trees that lined his shoulders had come undone when too much liquor later, the trees swayed relentlessly to and fro.

"You-you took me home!" said the director, the first time he'd seen me since.

"You couldn't take yourself home," I explained. "At one point, you tried to take a Tylenol and you couldn't open the container. It was one of those child-proof bottles."

"Oh," said the director, sending smoke and Southern Comfort into my ear. He had on another Hawaiian shirt so a figure on a surfboard rode the roll of flesh above his belt. "How old are you?"

"Sixteen," I said.

"Jesus Christ," said the director, his mouth falling open. "Did you take my clothes off?"

"Well, you couldn't, so yeah, I did."

"Oh, for fuck's sake," said the director, his fingers swimming through waves of silver hair.

"I didn't see your penis, if that's what you're worried about."

"Listen sweetheart, this isn't Last Tango in Calgary. Did we have sex or didn't we?"

"I don't think so," I said.

"You remember undressing me but you can't remember whether . . . Jesus, quit fucking with my head. Sex with you could land me in jail. I can see it now—from the Four Seasons to the Crowbar Hotel. This is great, fucking great."

"Hey, take it easy!" said the tequila drinker.

"Nothing happened. I'm sure," I said reassuringly.

"Yeah, you're probably right. If we'd had sex you'd know about it," said the director, a smile sliding to one side of his face.

"You know that plane that flew from Hawaii?" I said. "The one where pieces of fuselage fell away mid-flight. Well, some nights are like that,"

"Good point," said the tequila drinker. He ordered another tequila. "Wanna drink?" he said.

"Here's to crash landings!" he said when the drinks came. "What's your name anyway?"

"Cameo, as in the brooch," I said.

"Or a cameo role," he said. "My name's Sterling. As in the character."

"The character?" I said.

"A sterling character. I'm an actor. I think in terms of roles and characters."

TV serials and CBC movies are why I recognized him, although he seemed larger on screen. He said he was on location to play the part of a private eye, and now that he mentioned it, I could see him as a modem day Humphrey Bogart, He had the swagger, the voice that travelled a gravel throat.

"So what's your story?" he said. I tried to present my past in a neat package, but it veered from a tragedy to a comedy to a mystery where no one figures out anything.

"You know that fantasy?" he said, "the one about going out for a packet of cigarettes and never coming back? That's a big part of the actor's impulse, Every time I act, I run away, but it's structured, if you know what I mean. Anyone who says you can't run away from yourself is full of shit. You just run into someone else."

∾

Sterling was propped up on several pillows, smoking. "It's no way to live, trying to be perfect," he mused. "Fucking up is important too."

"What's in here?" I asked, examining a brown box.

"Alcohol, snack food and stuff. It's a miniature fridge." I looked around. His bathtub looked like a whirlpool, and the washbasin was hollowed out into the shape of a half shell. This hotel room was nothing like mine where the garbage can was starting to smell of something sinister. I was glad we'd decided on coming here.

"If you're hungry, we can get room service," he said as I opened a bag of pretzels.

"That's OK, I'm fine."

"Are you sure? You look kinda hungry."

When he smiled, the lines around his mouth pulled back like Venetian blinds. He had the look a camera loved—not the wholesome, all-American hunk kind, but something medieval. In the dark, the green light from a digital clock gilded his skin. He looked like one of the statues on the trophies I brought back from high school debating tournaments. My parents had persuaded me to join the debating club. "It'll help you think on your feet," my mother said. My father explained debating as a pre-pre law kind of experience—he had always wished for me the life of a lawyer. That way, everything I touched would turn to gold.

"To look at me now, I bet you'd never guess I was a debater," I said.

Sterling stirred in the darkness, "A debater?"

"Yeah, I was on the high school debating team. I spent all my spare time preparing myself for cross-examination. That's probably why I can't handle being cross-examined by counselors."

"Jesus," Sterling said, "when I was in high school, I spent all my spare time masturbating. The masturbator and the master debater — it's too poetic."

He curled around me and spoon-shaped we slept. Or rather, he slept. By now, my days and nights were completely reversed. I recalled Glenda's favourite song, "Walking on Sunshine." "I'm walking on sunshine," she always yodeled on the way to school. Glenda had a gaudy sunshine glamour that made each snowdrift glitter like the cheek of a cheap whore.

"You're leaking energy," said Sterling after I turned over several times.

"What do you mean?"

"Your legs, they won't stop moving."

"Can I turn on the TV?" I asked. "I'll put it on low."

"Sure," said Sterling. "Whatever you want."

I looked at the clock. It was approximately the time my mother used to pitter-patter into my bedroom, warbling "Rise and shine." Right now, she was probably sliding a knife around a blueberry muffin, coaxing it out of its tray. Then, she'd sit down at the kitchen table and write for a while. Before I left, she was working on a collection of short stories. *Mishaps* it was called. I found myself in several of the stories, transparently veiled by a different name. I bet she was spinning a story this very minute, and I would get caught in a mishap like a black fly. I suddenly felt incredibly tired. I wondered if my father was making coffee. The buzz of the coffee grinder, I could almost hear it.

When I woke in the late afternoon, the TV was still on. I reached for the remote control paddle and switched the channel to *Oprah*.

"Are the guests on *Oprah* actors?" I whispered in Sterling's ear.

"Probably," he said groggily.

The discussion on the talk show revolved around the difference between average and normal. There was a panel of psychologists which included someone who reminded me of Donna the counselor.

"Can anyone think of a pattern of behaviour that is average but not normal?" the psychologist asked.

"I match the colour of my underwear with my outfits," said a guest, looking concerned.

"Jesus Christ," said Sterling sitting up. He lit a cigarette.

"I'm glad you brought that up," said the psychologist. "That's a good example of behaviour that is normal but certainly not average."

"Is that normal?" Sterling asked.

"You're asking the wrong person," I said. "I own three pairs of underwear, and when they're dirty, I wear them inside out."

"I check my alarm clock a million times before I go to bed," said another guest. "I'm scared of waking up late. Then at work, I worry I left home without turning off the coffee pot. I think my house'll burn up, that I'll come home to no home at all."

"Believe it or not," said the psychologist, "that type of behaviour is common and thus average. However, it indicates the need for treatment, some kind of therapy. Good example."

"Psychologists make me sick," I said. "They pretend to know things they don't. They don't know that once you know too much, there's no way of going back. Why can't they understand that?"

"Yeah, well, trust your reactions," said Sterling. "There are limits to the intellect."

∾

I was running out of money, but Sterling said I could stay with him. After several days, I checked out of my hotel. I also called Glenda

"He says trust my reactions," I told her.

"Does he know how you react?" she said.

"He's an actor," I said, "a movie star. He's Canadian, but he lives in L.A. You've probably seen him on TV."

"Actors are sluts," Glenda said. "I hope you're using birth control."

"I stopped getting my period a long time ago, ever since I left home."

"Maybe you have endometrius," Glenda said.

"End-of-me-trius?"

"It's when your blood backs up into your body instead of coming out the normal way."

"You said my body wasn't a toilet," I said.

"It all depends how you use it," Glenda said.

According to Sterling, personalities could be gauged by the way people use their bodies. I became aware of his rhythms. His were slow and fluid, whereas I moved like a racehorse. "Relax," he always said, "give yourself over to the action."

One morning Sterling slept in.

"Cameo, where the hell's Sterling?" the director yelled into the phone.

"Right here," I said. "He's in bed."

"Tell him to get over here right away! We're shooting the pimp scene."

"The pimp scene?"

"Yeah, he's a pimp, I mean he plays a pimp."

"I thought he was a private eye."

"No. No. He's playing a pimp."

"Why would he lie to me?" I asked the director.

"I dunno. Private lies," he said.

"What's the movie about?" I said.

"Cameo, I don't have time for this shit."

"Tell me," I said. "Or I'll tell the cops we had sex. Then you'll be in shit for sure."

"Oh, for Christ's sake," he groaned. "O.K., it's about a runaway, if you really want to know. You needa script?"

"That's OK," I said. "I could probably write it."

It struck, a panic attack, like a pool cue in my stomach.

"So what?" Sterling said later, "I remake my personal life parallel to the fictional life I'm making." He lit a cigarette. "I told you, all actors are runaways. Your running away just became part of mine."

"But yours is structured." I imagined a trapezoid, a four-sided planal figure with two parallel lines. A decapitated triangle.

"Yeah, well, your little escape is structured too. You just don't know it."

"Quit fucking with my head," I said.

"'Tis the strumpet's plague to beguile many and be beguiled by one," Sterling said, putting on his Humphrey Bogart throat.

"I'm not a strumpet, and you're not the first person to beguile me," I said.

I started to throw my belongings into a garbage bag. "Where's my hairbrush?" I said, "Did you steal it?"

Sterling laughed. He lit another cigarette, and sat back to watch me. I tossed some small bottles of alcohol in with my clothes — room service had restocked the mini-bar. I found writing paper and a ballpoint pen in the dresser. I threw them in too.

"The pen," he said, "it's sticking out of the side of your bag." I looked down and, sure enough, the ballpoint pen had punctured the green plastic.

"So where ya headed?" he asked finally, his face curdling in the darkness.

# POLONAISE

FIONA FIRST LAID eyes on Ryszard when she was working at Crustacean Village, one of the many set ups in a large airy Toronto market.

"I want a lobster," he said with a thick accent.

She moved towards the tank. 'Which one?"

"Can you pick me one, one that will be good?"

She looked at him more carefully. His eyes seemed raw, stripped of something, prone to tears.

"Male or female?" she asked.

"I don't know. Please, could you pick me one?"

"OK," Fiona said.

He was obviously from elsewhere, and not accustomed to purchasing lobsters. She planned to give him a free placemat, a laminated piece of plastic with a diagram of a lobster, some facts about lobsters, and cooking instructions. Not that there was anything complicated about cooking a lobster, but there was no telling what some people might come up with.

Was he Hungarian? The week before, a Hungarian customer had told her Hungarian had no genders, no he's or she's. She'd mulled over this for hours. Certain things customers said changed the shape of her day. They planted themselves in her mind and grew leaves, a long stalk she could climb up when she had a few minutes of peace and quiet.

Fiona wrapped up the lobster and rang it in. "And, here's a free placemat," she said, rolling up the piece of plastic.

"Free?" He looked astonished.

"Yes," she said, smiling. "Compliments of — " She tried to find the right words. Of myself, would sound ridiculous. "The establishment."

"Ahhhhh," he said, "the establishment." He brushed away the brown bangs falling on his forehead and smiled. It was a sweet smile that involved the closing of his eyes for a split-second.

She watched him as he wandered off. He stopped in front of Ella's, the cheese stall across the way. For some reason, he cut a sad figure, standing in front of the papier-maché cow with her big grin and the bell around her neck.

The next day, he came back. He lined up behind an old lady who wanted five dollars worth of scallops. Fiona scooped up two handfuls and weighed them. "Is five dollars and thirty cents OK?" she said.

"Yes, dear," the old woman said, and clicked open her purse. Fiona's boss, throwing tiger shrimp on a bed of ice, nodded approvingly. He'd recently objected when he overheard her saying, "Is five dollars and eighty cents OK?" after a customer asked for six dollars worth of clams. Acknowledging it was difficult and time-consuming to put the exact dollar amount on the scale — to run back and forth adding another three clams or scallops or whatever it happened to be — he asked her to err on the side of more seafood rather than less.

He did some quick calculations — "Let's say one hundred and twenty customers a day ask for something by price rather than weight . . . twenty cents less than what they asked for means a loss of twenty-four dollars a day. Consider we could be making an extra twenty-four dollars a day if you give them twenty cents more, the difference is forty-eight dollars. It doesn't take a rocket scientist, Fiona."

"No, it doesn't," she agreed.

"Or someone with a history degree," he added to lighten things up.

Her history degree was a joke between them, ever since she applied for the job. With great formality, he'd asked her whether she had an interest in seafood. The interview took place in a back room where he was cutting up a swordfish. She admitted she didn't have an overriding interest in seafood, although she enjoyed eating it. Really, she was just looking for a job. She had just graduated with a degree in history and couldn't figure out what to do with it.

He said he appreciated her honesty.

"Figured out what to do with that history degree yet?" he asked her, every so often. Her boss was a practical man whose mind adhered to matters of substance—delivery orders, computer problems and his eldest son, a hulk in his late twenties he was extremely proud of, proud because this son was huge and had landed a lucrative job managing a warehouse in Vancouver.

"May I help you?" she asked Ryszard.

He peered into the lobster tank. "They are poor things, so good to eat, but really, they are poor things. Maybe, they think they are in a pet store and they are waiting for someone nice to take them home, pull off these things around their, what do you call these?" He snapped his hands a couple of times.

"Claws, we call them claws," said her boss impatiently. He looked anxiously at a young couple with a pram, approaching.

"They are waiting for someone to pull these things off their claws so they can be free and have some space to swim around, a box of their own with water."

"A tank, we call it a tank," Fiona volunteered.

"A tank of their own instead of crowded like this. Not knowing they will soon die."

"I don't think they think about those things," said Fiona. "Their nervous systems are very primitive."

"Look," said her boss testily, "Are you here because you're a member of one of these groups?"

"What group?"

"You know, one of these groups hell bent on saving the dolphins, saving the shellfish. 'Cause I'll tell you something, save too many dolphins and suddenly there's a shortage of certain fish."

That last comment, Fiona noticed, seemed for the benefit of the young parents who were now looking at the lobsters.

"No, I'm not part of this group. My name is Ryszard Spinalski."

"Oh," said her boss. He rubbed his big, thick hands together. "You came here to find her?" His voice shook a little.

"No, I came here to give this girl a ticket to my concert. Yesterday, she gave me a free . . . thing to put my lobster on."

"Placemat," said Fiona. "May I help you?" she asked the young parents.

"We haven't decided yet," the woman replied.

Her boss looked confused. He wiped his forehead with the back of his hand. "So you came here yesterday?"

"Yes."

"You came all the way from Poland to find Helena?"

"No, I came to Canada to give a concert."

"Would you wait a minute while I call her?" he asked Ryszard.

"Of course."

Her boss looked at his watch. "Fiona, I know you're off now, but could you work for ten more minutes?" He didn't wait for an answer but disappeared into the back room.

Fiona weighed five pounds of mussels for the young couple. They put the bag in the pram beside their sleeping a child and walked towards the stall where Hans, the German, sold homemade sausage.

Ryszard reached into the pocket of his grey blazer, whipped out the ticket, and presented it proudly.

She read the black print. SCHUBERT, CHOPIN. It figured. He didn't possess any of the telltale markings of a rock star-spiked hair, tattoos. He resembled a handsome, debonair college professor, the kind whose classes she used to enroll in, thinking if the guy turned out to be a complete drone, at least she had something pleasant to look at.

The date and time of his concert coincided with her best friend's birthday party, complete with male strippers. She apologized to Ryszard. She couldn't make it, and there was no point in wasting the ticket. But, she wished she could go. Wished very much she could go.

"This is not a problem," he replied. "You can come to my flat where I am staying, and I will play some pieces of my concert for you. What is your name and phone number? I will make you a call."

She wanted to reach out and help him step across a puddle of incorrect English usage. Instead, she ripped a piece of paper from a pad and grabbed a pen from a glass jar once filled with herring. What was the harm in going to his flat, and hearing a few tunes?

"You don't need to write it," he said. "Just tell me the number."

"Tell you the number?"

"I won't forget. I never forget numbers."

Fiona reeled off her phone number. He listened and effortlessly committed it to memory.

Her boss returned. He said his wife would like to see Ryszard, but next week some time. She was packing for a business trip to Vancouver, but she'd be sure to call him next Saturday and make arrangements. "What's the phone number of where you're staying?" her boss asked.

Fiona offered him the piece of paper she'd ripped off the pad, the pen still lying on the counter. Ryszard winked at her, pronouncing the numbers slowly, as her boss wrote them down with the same concentration he applied to taking down large orders.

He called her that same evening, as the sun was setting and people streamed along College Street, soaking up the cool after a steamy, smog-filled day. She recognized his voice, low and husky, misshapen by strange turns of phrase.

"It is Ryszard Spinalski. I am wishing to speak to a girl named Fiona."

"This is Fiona."

"Oh, hi, Fiona," he said, assuming a business-like tone. "This would be a good time to hear me play, if you would like a small concert. I am practising for my big concert and it would help me to have an audience. Perhaps you are free now or perhaps you are not. Perhaps you have an appointment with somebody else."

"No, I don't have an appointment."

"Good, where is your address? I will pick you up in a taxi and take you to this flat where I am staying."

"Where is this flat?" she asked, realizing she was already starting to change her way of speaking, like a new mother who fondles herself with baby talk.

She gazed out the window at a couple arm-in-arm, feasting on gelato in huge waffle cones. She'd rather go for gelato than listen to classical music — sit at an outdoor café and watch the parade of bodies. The colours in fashion that season were citrus. Women everywhere were barely clothed in lemony mesh and short skirts, orange sundresses with straps that crossed their shoulders at inventive angles.

He was staying on Havelock Street, not far from where she lived. She explained there was no need for a taxi. She looked at the clock on her wall. First she needed a shower because she still smelled of fish. She told him she'd be at his place in about an hour.

"I will be warming up," he replied.

"Warming up," she laughed. "When everyone else in Toronto is trying to beat the heat."

He emptied the last of a bottle of wine into her glass. "Fiona, if you were my neighbour and didn't know I was a musician who gave concerts, what would you think is my job?"

"I don't know," Fiona said.

"Guess, just guess," he almost pleaded.

"Mmmmmm," said Fiona, wracking her brain, "I would guess you were a dancer. You're so graceful."

"You are very kind," he said, laughing. "Very kind. I had a neighbour in Katowice. She didn't know I was a pianist. I practised everyday at the Academy. One day she appeared at my door and said a relative of hers had died. There would be a funeral and she needed flowers. She wanted to know the location of my shop."

"She thought you were a florist?"

"Very good!" he said, his eyes twinkling. "She saw me coming home after concerts, my arms full of flowers, going back to the car to bring in more flowers."

Fiona told him she'd never really listened to classical music before tonight. She'd always considered it funeral music, because it was serious and somber and the musicians dressed in black suits and dresses. And there was something else, but she couldn't remember what it was.

He looked shocked, as if she'd slapped him in the face.

She backtracked quickly, telling him that after hearing him play, her opinion had completely changed. Which it had. She'd never heard someone so good, let alone from several feet away. Sitting on the chaise lounge with her glass of wine, she'd forgotten the beautiful surroundings, the sculptures and expensive antiques; she'd become absorbed in a musical daydream, flowing from a melancholy state to one of anticipation, in which the music seemed to suggest a secret but then pull away from it, and after exploring other avenues, close in on it again, like a game of hide and seek. Parts of the Chopin made her think of flowers, and tinkling waterfalls.

"Well," he said, "Everyone thinks of flowers, but with Chopin, there are many gun shots behind the flowers. It's easier to hear if you're Polish."

"So it is funeral music?"

"Don't be silly," he said, flaring his nostrils. I don't know why you say it is funeral music. That is not a very intelligent idea." He walked through the living room and stepped out onto the balcony where he lit a cigarette and leaned against the iron railing.

She considered whether to let him stand out there, or to follow him onto the balcony and apologize, blame her stupid comment on the wine.

By way of a compromise, she stepped out on the balcony and asked him for a cigarette. "Of course," he said politely, but he seemed somewhat dejected.

She felt more secure, having something to hold onto to. She took a puff and exhaled dramatically into the darkness. Two more puffs, then she tapped the cigarette on the railing to remove the excess ash.

"I guess music appreciation isn't my bag." She hoped he would appreciate her honesty, as much as her boss had.

"Your bag? What do you mean, your bag?"

"My forte, it isn't my forte."

"Are you one of these people expecting everything to be happy? You want happy endings and happy music, maybe 'Twinkle Twinkle Little Star'?"

"No, oh my God, no. Well, yes, I do like happy endings."

He took the cigarette from between her fingers and threw it over the side of the balcony. He grabbed her hand and pulled her though the sliding door, back into the living room. What was he doing? she wondered, as he dragged her, as if she were a cart.

Maybe he was planning to throw her on the sofa and smother her in a passionate embrace. The tension had been building all evening. When he poured her wine, she could detect a pleasant scent from his neck, a combination of cologne and sweat laden with pheromones.

"You want 'Twinkle Twinkle Little Star', I will play you 'Twinkle Twinkle Little Star'."

"I don't want 'Twinkle Twinkle Little Star'!" He was treating her like a child, and now she sounded like a child — I don't want "Twinkle Twinkle Little Star". She might not be the most sophisticated listener, but she didn't deserve the indignity of being force-fed songs for toddlers.

He guided her towards the sofa and pulled her down on the soft, camel coloured pillows. Then he jumped back up, and marched towards the piano.

She stood up and pulled down her stretchy sundress. The high heel of her sandal caught on the fringe of the Turkish carpet. "I'm going home," she said.

"Going home? Why are you going home? I am going to play you 'Twinkle Twinkle Little Star'."

"I don't want to hear it."

"Why not? It comes from an 18th century French folk song called, well in English, it would be, 'I Will Tell You Mother'. Do you know this song?"

"No," said Fiona.

"I will sing to you this song in English."

She wanted to go home. She scanned the room for her purse, and spotted it where she'd dropped it, on the teak bookshelf. The wood had felt oily to the touch, not as oily as mackerel but greasier than the pine bookshelf she'd ordered from IKEA.

Ah, let me tell you, Mother,

What's the cause of my torment?

Papa wants me to reason like a grown-up

Me, I say that candy has

Greater value than reason.

His voice was deep and earnest. "That's the old folk song," he said. He was down on his knees in front of a shelf below a hi-fi system, pulling back a sliding door, to reveal a collection of record albums. The apartment belonged to a professor who taught music at the University of Toronto. "In Poland," he had said, "no professor could hope for a flat like this, with so many beautiful things, it is more than we can dream for."

Fiona sat down again. The nursery song had made her so sad that she started to cry. She was too old for this, but she couldn't help herself.

Ryszard came rushing over. "Honey, what is wrong? Is my singing so bad?"

She shook her head. "I'm twenty-seven and I feel so old. I spend my whole life with scallops and clams. I don't understand how I'm supposed to get from here to there, from scallops and clams to . . . "

"It is good to cry. Just cry. Would you like more wine, another cigarette?"

"Maybe later."

"Well, I think I need more wine." He walked to the liquor cabinet, pulled out another bottle, and opened it with a high-tech steel corkscrew that gleamed under the track lighting.

He returned to the sofa with his glass. "You are too young to be thinking this way. It is not good. Wait until you're forty. A friend of mine once said forty is a very hard border to cross, and so it is. When I was your age, I believed in the three 'M's in Polish — music, love and dreams. Now I believe in the three 'P's — alcohol, cigarettes and fucking."

Fucking. She didn't expect that word, but now she had to admit it — she'd sensed he'd fucked many women, women that came to his concerts and the receptions afterwards, women in low-cut black gowns, making eye contact as they bent over to pick up hors d'oeuvres. Whores D'oeuvres.

"Really," he said sadly, "forty is a hard border to cross. I turned forty-three today."

"Oh, my God! Happy Birthday!"

"Thank you," he said. "Why don't I play something to make you feel better?"

"That would be nice," she said.

But instead of sitting down at the piano, he walked back to the record albums, flipping through them until he found what he was looking for. He slipped the vinyl from its cover, and put it on the turntable.

The music that blared out of the speakers was formal and stately. It dredged up images of a ceremony with crowns and scepters, a king's court, a sinister event, such as an execution or an impending invasion by a foreign army.

"Guess who is the composer?" he asked, smiling.

"I don't know." She was embarrassed. She could probably tell Beethoven from Bach, but that was about it.

"It sounds like Wagner, yes?"

She nodded, recalling that certain people hated Wagner for the pomp and grandeur.

Suddenly, it all gave way to a simple theme, a piano playing "Twinkle Twinkle Little Star" very softly. Fiona laughed. "What is that?"

"It's by a Hungarian composer called Dohnanyi. It's called 'Variations on a Nursery Rhyme'. He wrote it as a joke. It jokes at composers of his time. He did not mean it to be rude. He wanted to bring people pleasure, to make them laugh. You like it?"

"I love it."


The hair was dagger straight, chemically bleached, and falling down to his waist.

"You like?" asked Zander, doing a twirl so his red skirt swished about his thighs.

"I love it, where'd ya rent that one?" asked Fiona.

"Wigs Are Us, on Bloor Street, in that tedious building across from The Great Canadian Bagel. The building is like totally boring, but the wig store is great."

"Happy B-day." She leaned over to kiss him, moving the platter of fish cakes she was holding to her left-hand side.

Lena was standing by the food table, popping brown balls of something into her mouth. She was a filmmaker who once told

Fiona she'd die if she couldn't make art. At one point, during their undergrad, they'd done lots of coffees and lunches with Zander. But then Zander dropped out of university, and Fiona and Lena realized he was really the sticky spread that held the two of them together.

Carlos had one arm on Gord's shoulder, and the other around Gord's waist, dancing to Elton John's "Candle in the Wind".

Zander rolled his eyes as they whirled by, Gord pinching Zander's ass. "Gourd," Zander groaned. "Squash."

Fiona handed Zander his birthday gift and went to the kitchen where she took the plastic wrap off the fish cakes. She carried the plate to the food table and set it down beside a black forest cake which reminded her of something she'd once heard — that Polish history is a dark dense forest in which it's easy to become lost.

A woman with enormous eyes, leaning against a pillar, said, "Do we really have to listen to this, a song about a dead actress?"

"It's better than the version he wrote for Princess Diana," someone piped up. "Goodbye, England's rose, or whatever it was."

"Why's he always writing songs for dead blonde women?" Lena said. "Don't you think that's kind of creepy?"

"Keith Richards asked the same question," said Zander, checking his makeup in the mirror above the mantelpiece.

"He did?" said Lena. "God, I can't believe me and Keith Richards think along the same lines. That's even more creepy." Lena picked up another brown ball and tossed it in her mouth.

"What is that?" asked Fiona.

"A meatless meatball."

Fiona hoped Lena wouldn't ask her what she was doing these days, so that she wouldn't have to admit she was still working at the fish place. The trick was to get Lena on the defensive first, talking about the films she started making but never quite finished.

"What film are you working on now, Lena?" Fiona asked

"Oh, it's this morality tale disguised as a hallucination. It was really taking off, but then I got distracted, I met this Polish guy and fell in love."

That's weird, I just met a Polish guy as well."

Lena beamed. "Aren't they romantic?"

"I don't know. I just met him. He's a friend of my boss's wife." Oh, no, she thought, she'd mentioned the fish store.

"What does this guy do?" Lena asked.

"He's a concert pianist."

Lena's jaw dropped. She turned slightly pale.

"What?" said Fiona. "What?"

"You're dead. You're dead meat."

"I am?"

"Well, yeaahh," said Lena. "Think about it. If he's anything like my Pole, he's totally romantic, but yours is a pianist on top of it. Because he's an artist, he's probably not emotionally charred. He's come to terms with his feminine side, so he's not walking around trying to be a man. There's nothing worse than a man who tries to be a man. You always have the sense something is missing."

Zander was gazing in the mirror, reapplying his lipstick.

"I'm totally confused," said Fiona.

"That's OK. It's OK to be confused. Life is confusing."

Zander sashayed over, grabbed Lena from behind and kissed her neck. "Fiona, you're not drinking anything," he said critically. "What can I get you?"

"A martini?" said Fiona. "I need to prepare myself for those male strippers."

"Sure thing," said Zander, slipping away.

"I bet he drinks," said Lena.

"Who?"

"Your Polish guy. It's cultural thing, goes way back."

"Now that you mention it," said Fiona, thinking of the night before, "yeah, he drinks like a fish. He did the other night anyway."

"Are you still working at that fish place?"

"I'm kind of nervous about these male strippers," said Fiona, changing the subject. "I have this really bad habit of taking people's clothes off with my eyes, but I don't like them doing it for my entertainment."

"I know what you mean. Remember the last ones?"

Gord appeared over Lena's shoulder. "I do," he said. "I felt like the wolf who cried boy."


There was a laminated card in the middle of the table, by the white ceramic ashtray. She picked it up and read it. Ryszard had gone inside to use the washroom. The card gave a brief history of gelato — its origins in Italy — then detailed the difference between ice-cream and gelato, the nebulous territory between gelato and sorbet. It all had to do with amounts of butterfat, artificial and natural flavors.

Fiona like the definition of gelato the best — In Italy, gelato means frozen, but the word has evolved to mean frozen pleasure.

It would be nice, she thought, if you could freeze pleasure, such as the last half hour, and thaw it out, experience it again whenever you pleased.

She loved outdoor cafés. Ryszard had charmed the waitress with his exquisite manners. It seemed, as Zander would say, he had the world by the balls. His concert had been a success, and from time to time, he treated the table like a keyboard, tapping finger patterns with his right hand while he talked.

He described Poland, its castles, churches, and famous salt mine . . . how the borders of Poland had changed over the years, which he illustrated, using a napkin he'd spread out on the table.

He made Poland sound like the promised land. He said she should really come to visit. He would show her Europe's best-kept secret, the city of Krakow, so historic no skyscrapers are allowed.

Check for the wedding ring, Lena had advised. She said Eastern European men wear it on their right hand, and unless he's a complete loser, which he obviously isn't, he's probably married. Lena's problem was that her Polish lover was married. He'd married obscenely young. His wife, a staunch Catholic, refused to give him a divorce. Somewhere between too many martinis and the arrival of the strippers, Fiona had forgotten the details.

Ryszard returned to the table with a bouquet of flowers, a blur of pastel daisies. He proffered them, bowing slightly.

"Thank you," she said. "How did you get them?" She wasn't accustomed to such displays. She'd heard somewhere it was easier to be on the giving rather than the receiving side of love. To leave someone rather than be left. The same, she supposed, applied to flowers.

"The waitress showed me out the side door," said Ryzsard impishly.

I bet she did, thought Fiona.

Ryszard sat down in his chair and pulled out a pack of cigarettes. The night before she'd noticed a tobacco stain on his front tooth, but it had since disappeared.

"How do you know my boss's wife?" Fiona asked. She wasn't sure how to broach the subject of his marital status without sounding as if she was looking for a husband.

His face darkened. "Mmmmm, my grandmother saved Helena's mother's life during the war."

"Oh."

"You know Helena's Jewish?"

"No. I didn't know," said Fiona.

He looked slightly pained. 'Well, she is. And, soon she will die, if she's not careful."

"Why will she die?"

"Her family owned a big building in Poland, a building with a lot of flats in it where many people live. She made a visit to Poland to try and own this building again. To get it, she has to come back, but the people in the building know she wants it and will murder her.

"Murder her?" Are they crazy?"

"No, they are not crazy," said Ryszard. "It happens all the time. Jews come back to try and get a building they owned, and people kill them. They are found dead in the river."

Fiona was appalled. "That's horrible."

"It's not so horrible."

"But it's murder!" she said.

Ryszard nodded. "Yes, it's murder."

Fiona couldn't believe it. She felt as though she'd entered a thick, foreboding forest to find a house with a man whom she believed to be as harmless as her grandmother, but who was only pretending. In reality, he was a wolf masquerading as a grandmother, an anti-Semitic canine.

"You are like my mother," he said kindly. "She didn't believe in murder either. She didn't like Jews, but she was very Catholic. She risked my life, her life, my father's life, my sister's life to hide five Jews. She told my father to build a wall in front of a wall in the barn, and that's where she put them."

He lit his cigarette and inhaled deeply. "My father, he didn't mind the Jews, but he didn't think she should risk our lives to save them. Anyway, only Helena's mother survived. The others went to Krakow thinking they could escape and were murdered."

Fiona put a spoonful of mango gelato in her mouth. "That's so bizarre. That your mother didn't like Jews, but took incredible risks to save them."

"Well," said Ryszard, "when she was hiding the Jews, my mother started to like them. Maybe because she was saving them and bringing them food, and they were very nice. But, in the end, she didn't like them anymore."

"Why not?"

"It doesn't matter." He flicked his hand dismissively.

Fiona felt offended, as though they were strolling down a path together, and he'd suddenly decided enough was enough. He crushed his cigarette in the ashtray. His face was covered in a light sweat, as if someone had spritzed him, like a vegetable in the produce section, to keep him fresh. His black jeans and polo shirt probably weren't helping, attracting the sun and making him hotter than need be.

She wanted to continue the conversation. But she knew better than to push. It could take a bad turn, make a mess of what for the most part, had been a pleasurable day.

Fiona woke up to the three dark hairs on Ryszard's right shoulder blade. He slept like a shrimp, curled up, but not too tightly, on his left side. She pulled away from him, realizing it was Food Bank day and she had to get a move on to make it there by eight-thirty.

Her clothes from the night before lay cast adrift on the couch in the living room. She grabbed them and headed for the bathroom, a large glittery room that looked out on to the tangle of garden below. A quick shower was in order — not that anyone at the food bank would be fragrant and well groomed.

When she returned to the living room, dressed, and with her hair twisted into a wet rope, Ryszard was sitting the balcony, wrapped in a crimson bathrobe, a glass in one hand, his legs slightly apart, smoking a cigarette.

She blew him a kiss and began sifting through the kitchen cupboards for plastic bags from the grocery store, or better still, from the liquor store because they were stronger and could hold more weight.

As she folded up the bags neatly like pillow cases, her lover, her lover — she relished the-pulled-from-the-underground steamy sound of the word — stepped onto the cool ceramic tiles, and watched her sharp movements with amusement. He asked her fondly what she was doing.

She told him she had to run an errand, which would take several hours, after which she'd come back, because today was her day off. That's if he wanted. Perhaps, it was better to stay away for a while, to savor what had happened, to let the events take on a blurry edge rather than re-insert them so soon into the confines of reality.

"I am going with you," he said.

"Oh, no, you can't. Believe me, where I am going is not a place you want to go."

"Why not?"

"It's depressing," she said. She glanced at her watch. Arriving later than eight-thirty meant purgatory — an excruciating wait rather than a very long wait.

"It's not the kind of thing two people who have just slept together should do the next morning."

"And what should these two people sleeping together do the next morning?"

Wasn't it obvious? These two people who have just slept together should go back to bed, flounce around on the pillows, gnaw at each other's bodies and then, stunned from pleasure, go to an outdoor café for coffee and croissants.

"If there is something you need to do, I want to come."

"Look, Ryszard, what I have to do is terribly unpleasant. I have a sister, she's very ill, and I help her out by going to get her food. She can't do it for herself."

"Oh, that's bad. But I like shopping, looking at the things for sale."

"I'm not going shopping. I'm going to a place that hands out free food to poor people. It's horrible and depressing."

"I want to come and see this place," said Ryszard, his voice a bit petulant. "So it doesn't have the smell of money. I don't care."

He had no idea what he was in for — the throng of bodies as the grimy clock on the food bank wall neared eight-thirty, the dashing across the room to grab numbers from a small cardboard box, often upended in the process. Nine o'clock rolls around, and the woman hunkered down behind the desk, starts calling numbers in a sharp staccato, demanding health cards, and signed letters from those not well enough to pick up foodstuffs for themselves.

Fiona always brought along a book. But the room was usually cold, the chairs uncomfortable, and people were constantly hacking and coughing — and it never failed, there'd be one larger-than-life person who made reading impossible. One week, it was a woman who insisted on pontificating about birthday cakes — telling how last week, she'd called ahead of time for a birthday cake, and even though her husband said it was impossible, she took the cake down to the grocery store where it was made — the label is on the plastic cover, so you know — and told them it came from the food bank, and the people working in the bakery department said it was possible to write her kid's name with piped icing on the frosting, and they even put on a couple of those rosebuds.

It was bad — the collection of disabled, mentally ill, or just impoverished, but most of all, the long wait, longer than it had to be, thanks to the director. Glenn, obviously retired, was an amalgam of zeal and announcement fervor. He made the announcements before the volunteers started guiding people, one by one, according to their numbers, into a larger room where everyone, supervised closely, picked two items from each shelf of dented canned meat, dented canned vegetables, dented soup. There were also bags of pasta, cereals, jars of jam and peanut butter, bread and baked goods, all dangerously close to their expiry dates.

Glenn's announcements revolved around the importance of bringing your own plastic bags and calling ahead for diapers and birthday cakes. They had the tendency to bleed into sermons. He talked about the importance of counting one's blessings, such as living in the wonderful country of Canada, having food banks, willing volunteers, and the love of God. Finally, he wound up his sermon up by inviting 'the believers' to take part in a prayer. This delayed the whole process by another fifteen minutes, so it was close to ten before things actually got under way, before the person with the number one started circling the food room, plucking from the shelves the cans with the least external damage.

Well, she thought, after what Ryszard described last night, sipping on chilled vodka — how he'd grown up, under the slate gray awning of communism, standing for hours in front of stores in long line-ups and then crossing the threshold to find the shelves empty — maybe he wouldn't find a trip to the food bank so odious.

The string of bells on the front door clinked as Ryszard pushed it open. When they entered the faded room, Fiona gasped. Except for the woman who jotted down health card numbers, the room was empty, with rows and rows of vacant chairs.

"We're closed today," the woman said from behind her desk. "We're having a citrus drive. A fund raiser."

Fiona could see through to the food room where cardboard boxes filled with oranges were stacked on the floor.

"Glenn gave the dates the food bank would be closed," said the woman, "in his announcements, but maybe you didn't hear him. There's some stuff in those boxes on the chairs by the wall. Bread and stuff, delivered today. Help yourself."

Fiona thanked the woman and walked over to check out the boxes. Ryszard followed close behind. One box contained bread, dry white loaves shaped like footballs in paper bags, some broken baguettes, but also some organic bread, soft and meaty, preserved well in tight cellophane.

She picked out two loaves and stuffed them into one of the bags she'd brought. On a regular food bank day, the good loaves would be gone by person number three. The next box really set a precedent. It contained a bag of baby carrots, heads of Boston butter lettuce, Swiss chard, bunches of fresh dill and rosemary.

This is very good food," said Ryszard, as she hastily filled two more bags.

"It isn't always like this, trust me," she whispered.

Hearing Glenn's voice, she turned around. He glanced at Fiona and smiled. He obviously recognized her. There had been times when annoyed by his blessings, she had read her book, looking up at him occasionally, so as not to appear completely rude. He crossed the room and explained that the food bank was closed for a week. Then he asked her if she could make it through until Monday. Fiona explained she hadn't come here for herself, but for her sister who was very ill. Glenn said he'd have someone put together a few bags of canned goods from the other room, which unfortunately she couldn't enter, as volunteers were busy packing oranges.

Fiona thanked him very much. Already, she felt more kindly disposed towards him because he knew that like him she was a helper rather than a parasitic member of society trying to get as many freebies as possible. Not that everyone who came to the food bank was a parasite, but she wondered about the ones she'd heard admonished by the woman at the desk for coming too often. There was a teenager in an expensive leather jacket and beautiful boots who breezed into the food bank as if it was a convenience store. Fiona imagined the girl had left home, was living in a house with several rebellious boys her own age, and used the food bank to cut corners.

But, then again, Fiona had to acknowledge, she wasn't a natural born helper. She helped her sister, but she wasn't the kind of person who'd make a good nurse or social worker, or who got satisfaction from volunteer work. Glenn was another story and she'd known others like him, who devoted their lives to good causes, and to helping the unfortunate; she'd often suspected that they were engaged in a co-dependent relationship with the needy. This was of a different order from Ryszard's grandmother who hid Jews, risking the lives of those she cared most about. There was a difference between helpers and heroes, she mused.

It seemed a good time to introduce herself, as Glenn didn't know her by name. She also introduced Ryszard. It gave her pleasure to say that he was a concert pianist from Europe. She'd bet a million clams Glenn had never had a concert pianist within these four walls.

Ryszard shook Glen's hand, and then launched into the same kind of monologue he'd directed at the waitress at the cafe. But, whereas he'd expressed his delight at the pleasant surroundings of the outdoor patio, he now focused on what a wonderful service Glenn was providing. He said that in Poland, people wouldn't believe there was such a place as a food bank, where people can go and get food when they're hungry. He said he'd seen many wonderful things in Toronto, but this food bank was the most wonderful.

Glenn beamed. He gave Ryszard a history of the food bank, which Fiona hadn't realized was different from the metro food banks. He said he'd started this food bank himself. The idea had come to him one evening, while he was lying in bed, listening to the radio with earphones because his wife was trying to sleep. He'd heard about a woman in New York who'd sensed a need for a different kind of food bank, where people could choose items for themselves, rather than having bags of food packed for them.

And, whereas most food banks had little variety (deliveries of hundreds of jars of pickles, for instance, from one store), she dreamed of one that involved a lot of organizations, and could offer a wide array of food. Glenn decided right then to start a similar food bank in Toronto. Ryszard listened in amazement.

"My wife did many good things," he said, "before she died of a cancer. She lived to serve others. She made soup for the sick woman down the road. She did things for the church, and so much for her mother and our children. My wife never stopped moving. She was a perpetuum mobile."

"She was what?" Glenn asked.

"Perpetuum mobile. She used to get very angry with me because I am the type of person who can sit and smoke and think for hours without doing anything."

Fiona looked at Ryszard's ears, as small as shells, and his serious mouth. He appeared so vulnerable. She could imagine the scenes from his life so clearly already, had glanced at a photo of his wife, a woman with short grey hair, her chin raised, a stony expression conveying arrogance.

Yes, she could picture everything. Ryszard, sitting and smoking, steeped in melancholy, or running over a piece of music in his mind; and, his wife, a powerhouse of energy, with a straight back, demanding he get out of the chair and do something.

"If music were the food of life," he said wistfully, "I could feed so many people."

"You could always play to raise money for charity," Glenn suggested.

Ryszard looked a bit confused. He said he'd never heard of such a thing in Poland. Musicians gave concerts for free, at the academy or in the park. He wasn't sure people would pay to hear music if they didn't have to, as most of them were poor and just scraping by.

It had been years since she'd sat on a concrete slab, outside Sidney Smith Hall. Students passed by, locked up their bikes to trees in the clutch of summer. Back then, she was always scribbling — dates of wars, the beginning and end of exams, deadlines for papers — contemplating whether to ask a certain professor for an extension.

He was probably on vacation. She picked up her purse and entered the building, slowly climbing the stairs she used to run up in a mad panic. In the hallway of the history department, she stopped several times, reading notices, looking at cartoons and newspaper articles tacked to the bulletin boards. She tapped lightly beneath his name engraved on a plaque. When he opened the door, his eyes widened with surprise.

"Fiona, long time, no see. To what do I owe this pleasure?"

"Hello, Dr. Goodman, I wonder if I could ask you a question."

"Well, of course, come in."

He offered her a chair, not the uncomfortable plastic one she used to sit in when she was discussing essay topics, but the black leather recliner. It seemed in her absence she'd graduated to the more comfortable chair.

"If you'd like a letter of reference, I'd be glad to write one," he offered, sensing her hesitation.

"No, it's not that."

She perused his bookshelves, the photos in copper frames gracing his desk, his wife in shorts with a tennis racket, his daughter Tova.

"Mmmmm," she said, "I remember you once said that Polish history is a dark dense forest in which it's easy to get lost, and, well, I met this Polish guy . . . "

"And you're lost?" he said.

He made coffee, heating water on a hot plate, pouring it through a paper filter while Fiona recounted the conversation she'd had with Ryszard. At one point, he stopped her to ask a question.

"Did he say 'it's OK to murder Jews'?"

"I don't know if those were his actual words, but he didn't seem to think it was terribly wrong."

When Fiona had finished, she waited nervously for Professor Goodman to announce a verdict. But he didn't.

"Fiona, Polish-Jewish relations are very complicated. It would take me a long time even to begin to explain them . . . but what you have to understand is that life is cheap in Eastern Europe. It's very different from here. There, you have tenants in a building they've lived in most of their lives. It's not like here, where people just rent apartments for a short time and then move somewhere else. So, if a stranger comes and lays claim to an apartment building, that amounts to putting all the tenants out on the street. Anti-Semitism is alive and well in Poland, I'd be the first to say it. But, I'm not sure the situation is as simple as murdering a Jew, or the way we'd see it anyway. People are struggling to survive, and as I said, things are different over there. For them, violence and oppression have been a way of life for a very long time." He handed her a cup of coffee and continued.

"As for his mother disliking Jews and hiding five of them, well, that's an old story . . . but, Fiona, if you have all these questions, why don't you just ask him? Do you suspect he's an anti-Semite?"

"I'm not sure."

"Does he know you're Jewish?"

"No, I haven't told him."

Professor Goldman sighed.

"I will ask him," she said.

But she knew it was too late.

She'd already entered the dense foreboding forest, and gone too far along the twisting and turning path to turn around now and run back towards the sunlight.

# Freedom Holes

Door to door, nothing goes by its real name. For example, Mickey has instructed me never to use the word 'flyer'. A flyer is not a flyer. It's a promotional booklet filled with coupons from Pizza Sensation and a car dealership. We're not drifting around the outer reaches of Halifax, knocking on doors. No, we've landed like members of the military at a training field, where there are strict rules to ensure as many hits as possible. Our lives depend on these hits, because we work for commission. If we sell $24.99 worth of booklets, nine dollars is ours.

Or perhaps I'm mistaken. Mickey is Mickey. He probably goes by his real name. He sat beside me on a garden chair in the back of a dilapidated van headed for the training field. He slurped coffee from a paper cup and laughed at the lewd jokes made by other members of the training crew. At one point, he pulled out a map, and said he'd be training me.

One boy, in his early twenties, didn't even make it to the training field. The minute his trainer showed him the booklets, he demanded to be let out of the van. He said he had another job where he made ten dollars an hour and he didn't need this kind of shit. The van pulled to the side of the road, and the boy disappeared into a grove of trees.

"It's my livelihood, and he calls my job shit," complained the trainer who was supposed to be training the young boy. "Like hell, he makes ten dollars an hour." Mickey laughed. "Doin' what? Givin' blow jobs?"

All the trainers gave guffaws of emotional support. I was the only woman in the van, and it seemed risky to laugh along. I've succumbed to such smiles in the company of men, but not the likes of the driver, the trainers and the two straggly young boys sitting on the floor strewn with candy wrappers and crushed coffee cups.

"Is there anything beside me?" the driver asked the trainer in the passenger seat. For the first time, I noted the lack of side-view mirrors. The engine backfired. "Sawed-off cocksucker!" the driver shouted.

Five minutes, later, the van stopped, and one of the straggly young boys along with a trainer hopped out. They dismounted like angular cowboys and disappeared into a ditch.

I feel as though I've been dropped out of the sky. Yesterday, I had a job interview with a man in an expensive business suit who perused my resume. His name was Tim.

"OK, Virginia, what would you consider your biggest weakness?"

That stumped me. I thought of all my weaknesses, trying to think which one would appear most attractive to a prospective employer.

"I'm a perfectionist. Sometimes it gets in the way of things."

Tim nodded and wrote something down on a pad. I gazed at a poster of a Hawaiian pizza behind his head. It made me hungry, the chunks of pineapple and ham poking out of a warm blanket of cheese. Maybe I would be asked to come up with an idea for a poster or a billboard, when I advanced. The ad in the newspaper said *opportunity for advancement,* and I planned to advance as soon as possible, if Tim hired me.

According to Mickey, Tim makes $300,000 dollars a year, and he started where I'm starting right now. Somehow I can't imagine Tim standing with Mickey in a subdivision of Halifax in the driving rain. As a matter of fact, I can't imagine Tim standing with Mickey anywhere. Mickey is an eyesore with sunken cheeks, missing teeth and a stained orange baseball jacket. I have no way of guessing his age. He looks like a rummy-dummy, in recovery from something he'll never quite recover from.

He tells his life like a success story. It would make me sad if the sun was shining, but it makes me even sadder in the rain with his map and the promotional coupons getting soaked. A year ago, he felt a hundred years old, but now he feels twenty-five. He works for himself in the fresh air, and there's no boss watching over him.

When Tim's secretary phoned to say I'd been selected, she said tomorrow I'd be meeting with clients and to dress appropriately. I could kill myself for wearing the leather pumps I save for special occasions. The rain has already permeated the leather and dampened my socks. My only consolation is that my brother is wandering around Afghanistan in green camouflage that was never designed for a hot climate. He's roasting like a suckling pig, because nobody thought to order gear for the desert.

After several women have slammed the door on us, we dive into a wooded area behind a line of houses. Mickey lights a cigarette by creating a cave around the flame with his left hand. He inhales deeply and then coughs, and hacks a wad of mucous onto a maple leaf glossy with wetness. Now that he's working, he says his ex-wife has let him move into her basement with wood paneling, a cot, and wall-to-wall carpet. Sometimes she comes and sits on the edge of his cot, and they share a cigarette and talk about stuff.

I pull out my thermos that resembles a bullet, unscrew the lid and pour several shots of inky Columbian. I empty the cup in two gulps. The caffeine rips through my system.

"OK," says Mickey, "A.A."

I wonder if he is going to tell me about Alcoholics Anonymous. My brother, the one in Afghanistan, spent a winter attending A.A. meetings. He had to write a three-page emotional inventory. It's the only soul-searching he's ever done, at least to my knowledge, and he was proud of it. He read it to me in his bedroom, the sun streaming through the window, the melt water in the gutter providing a soft accompaniment. *Now that the drinking-worrying-insanity cycle seems to be broken by some sobriety and more serious thinking along the lines that AA encourages, I still have to break the hold of anxiety about the failure overwhelming the present and distorting everything. It is still very hard to look ahead and not feel great panic over what •will happen.*

"In our company," Mickey says, "it stands for — achieve a positive attitude, maintain a positive attitude."

I can't figure out what the two 'A's stand for. Wouldn't A.M. be better? A for achieve, and M for maintain. But, I'm not about to ask. Questions raise the suspicion that you have a type A personality — instead of just following orders, you want to know what's going on. The problem is, half the time the people giving orders don't know what's going on either.

"Then there's B.B," he continues. "Be prepared. Be on time. C.C. Take control and remain in control. K.K. Know what you're selling and why you're selling it."

He has told me to observe for at least three hours until I get the hang of things.

We leave the woods and go back to where we left off. We walk up a sidewalk together, but I stand to one side while Mickey rings the door bell. I point to a sign by the mailbox that reads NO SOLICITORS.

"Just watch," he says with authority.

A woman answers the door, wearing a housecoat and holding a paperback novel with the title CUBA embossed on a cover that reflects like tinfoil. I wonder what her life consists of, that she's still in her housecoat well past noon. Perhaps she works nights.

"Don't worry," Mickey tells her, "I ain't here sellin' religion. I'm here on behalf of Taylor/Ford to offer you a free oil change."

"It's free?"

Mickey flashes the booklet, and explains that the purchase would make her eligible for various discounts — on a lube job, a tire rotation, and a free oil change.

"Oh, I don't know," the woman sighs. "My husband usually deals with those things."

"And when will your husband be home?"

"Well," she says, brushing a blonde curl back from her face. "It just depends."

"Depends on what?" asks Mickey, his voice flecked with aggression.

"His working schedule." I notice the way she says this. 'His working schedule', as if those words were inflated with air and could take off at any moment.

"Will he be home by seven?" Mickey inquires.

"He might be."

Then Mickey tries to ply her with Pizza Sensation coupons. Personally, I would have retreated after *He might be*. There's a fine line between encroaching on someone's privacy and harassment. Mickey, however, careens on with his spiel, oblivious to fine lines.

"No thanks, I don't eat cheese. I have an allergy to cheese."

"What about your kids? They must like a pizza from time to time."

"They do," the woman concedes, "but not that many pizzas."

"How many pizzas, let's say over a year?" Mickey asks.

"Jesus Christ, I don't know, maybe eight."

"That's great!" says Mickey. "If you buy this booklet, you pay two dollars less on eight regular pizzas and then you get a free pizza."

"I'm sorry," says the woman, shutting the door. "I'm not interested." The jacket on her book announces "Dramatic, diverting action!" and "The Explosive *New York Times* bestseller."

I think sadly of the last two years I devoted to trying to write stories.

Back then I lived with a silver-haired man, an engineer with a sweet demeanour who supported my writing habit. I met him in a trendy downtown Halifax bar where the waiters called themselves artists, another way of saying (I soon realized) that they were just doing their own thing—making jewelry out of silver spoons, playing in alternative rock bands, following their friends around with video cameras. A waitress with blonde spiky hair baked pornographic gingerbread men she decorated with chocolate sprinkles and piped icing—gingerbread cowboys in hats and boots, bent over, studded with inedible silver beads.

If I had met Elmer in any other environment, I doubt I would have described myself as a writer. After all, I hadn't published a thing. I carried *Best American Short Stories* around like a bible in my rucksack and scribbled bits of dialogue in notebooks while drinking coffee in the cafés along Spring Garden Road, but that was about it. My lack of credentials was of no concern to Elmer, however. He was a senior engineer who worked in the offshore oil industry and brought home a healthy paycheck every two weeks. The declaration that I was a writer he interpreted, I guess now, more as an admission of guilty passion, than a form of self-aggrandizement.

For the two years I lived with Elmer, I composed furiously, sending out stories to journals that rejected them with quaint justifications, something about not meeting their needs. I joined the Writer's Federation, went to meetings. At one of them, a writer in her fifties stood up and said, "I can't think of any other business in which people set themselves up for so much rejection." Everyone in the room applauded. But now I know that woman was wrong. Writers only stand in rejection's shadow. To experience true rejection is to walk around door-to-door, driving a stake through people's peace and quiet in order to drum up enough money for a meal at the end of the day.

We retreat down the steps, Mickey preoccupied with a piece of foolscap attached to a clipboard. "Look," he says. He's drawn a rough sketch of the neighborhood — an outline of a house representing each house. Two slanted lines indicate a roof, three lines for two sides and a foundation. Several of his houses have an X inside, whereas others are empty of markings. The last house has a dot inside.

Mickey explains this is his way of keeping track because later on, we're going back to all the houses where no one answered the door and all the houses that were a maybe. The houses with an X mean the people said no. The empty houses mean no one was home. The houses with the dot represent a maybe. "We just got a maybe," he said, gesturing to the house with the woman allergic to cheese.

"*That* was a maybe?" It seemed as clear-cut a case of "no" as I've ever witnessed.

"Of course it was a maybe! The woman said her husband would be back later in the evening. We have to swing by around seven and see if he wants the free oil change. The maybe's are the most valuable."

How can a maybe be more valuable than a yes? Perhaps it's the thrill of the hunt. I look at my watch. It's eleven in the morning. My mind seizes up. I can't imagine eight more hours of wandering this neighbourhood. With each house, I have to fight my urge to run away. I lack Mickey's sense of entitlement, his assurance that he's entitled to march up people's sidewalks and harass them with two sets of promotional coupons, and now I realize, sometimes twice in a day. When he rings the doorbell,

I cringe. I come from a clan that believes such intrusions on one's privacy are unconscionable and should be outlawed, a clan that sprays these home invaders — the telephone solicitors and door-to-door salespersons— with noxious requests, statements, witty repartee. *What's your home phone number? I'll call you back sometime around midnight when I'm not busy.*

It occurs to me that I've become 'the other,' the enemy. In my desperation, I've become a terrorist, and now I'm engaged in internal warfare. I hear my mother's voice. *You have to start somewhere.* As if all somewheres lead to a better place. But what choice do I have? In the last three months, all prospective employers have turned me down, slammed the door in my face.

I follow Mickey up the next sidewalk. No one answers the door. We make our way up more sidewalks, ring doorbells, buzz buzzers to no avail. Mickey draws more empty houses on his map.

Finally, a beautiful woman in a sarong answers the door. The cloth intimates a narrow waist and breasts that seem almost architectural. "Hello?" she says. She eyes Mickey with mild confusion. Her eyes dart from the strands of gray hair plastered across his forehead to his orange baseball jacket and then to his muddy sneakers.

"Don't worry, I ain't here sellin' religion," Mickey jokes.

"I'm sorry. I don't understand."

"My name is Mickey," says Mickey with bravado. "I'm here on behalf of Taylor/Ford to offer you a free oil change."

The woman suddenly assumes a serious expression. Her eyes cloud with distance. She points a jeweled finger at the NO SOLICITORS sign on the mailbox.

My mind slows down, as if I were drugged. I wanted this to happen. When I was writing short stories, there were certain things I didn't know would happen. They seemed to arrive from somewhere else. Only when I was in the middle of writing a story, did I realize a certain thing had happened, that I had actually wanted it to happen, like an orphan who shows up on your doorstep and says *You may not know me, my name is Rachel, but you have always known me and your name is Rachel too.*

Mickey barrels on. "See, what happened is I rang the doorbell and *then* I saw the No Solicitors sign. So, I figured it wouldn't be polite to run away."

The woman looks at me, and I make an attempt to smile. She looks back to Mickey. Her upper lip wavers. "Please go, and never come back." It sounds more like a request than an order.

She closes the door and stands behind it, eyeing us through two panes of glass. Mickey draws a house with X inside on his map. He approaches the next house, a bungalow, ranch style with low-pitched roofs and a carport. Shrubs manicured into round globs guard the doorstep. He ambles up the sidewalk, while I walk despondently behind him, contemplating the state of my shoes.

He rings the doorbell. It provokes a manic barking from inside. I keep my hood up, and wrap my arms around my body to preserve body heat. I wish I could run away, but where to? I'm not sure buses even run in these subdivisions. I don't have enough money for a taxi.

A dog finally answers the door, or that's the way it appears. A beautiful German shepherd leaps on Mickey, nearly knocking him over. "Stella, sit!" laughs a young woman with long dark hair. The dog sits, wagging its tail frantically.

"She's only two," the woman says. "It's the terrible twos." I gaze at her long legs in tight jeans, the elasticized belt with a buckle in the shape of a butterfly. "May I help you?"

The dog-do has obviated the need for Mickey's ' I ain't here sellin' religion' line. He launches right into his presentation.

She's not really listening. She's preoccupied with Stella, whose head she strokes continually. "Well," she says, "I have a mechanic I've been dealing with for years."

"Oh," says Mickey. "Do you like pizza?"

"Sure," says the woman.

"I've a great deal, here," says Mickey, pulling out a book of Pizza Sensation coupons.

"Well, we get pizza from Gia's pizza. We like a really thin crust."

"Pizza Sensation has a thin crust pizza," Mickey says. "There's a vegetarian pizza with purple onion."

"Well, we're pretty loyal to Gia's pizza," the woman says. "They have goats cheese. I love goats cheese." She eyes Stella who is wandering around the steps.

"You have your choice of three toppings, including the purple onion," Mickey says, "So you could order a thin crust pizza with purple onions, green peppers and olives."

"Do they have goats cheese? Do they infuse their olive oil with garlic?"

"No, they don't have goats cheese," Mickey says. "They use mozzarella, but it seems as though you and your husband eat a lot of goats cheese and a change is as good as a rest."

"A change is as good as rest," repeats the woman. "Where's this Pizza Sensation located?"

"In Halifax, on Agricola Street."

"The fact is," says the woman, pausing, "my husband and I don't get into Halifax much."

"You must get into Halifax, sometime!" Mickey insists.

I realize Mickey is a natural born salesman. I would have admitted defeat when the woman mentioned olive oil infused with garlic. To his credit, he is training me to the best of his ability. "OK," he says, as we head to the next house, "remember what I said about A.A. What else? If you dress well, you feel better about yourself, and if you feel better about yourself, you sell more. Another thing, you have to have sex with your customers."

So this is it, I think. The company is a front for a prostitution ring. But, no, that's not it. Mickey isn't pimp material, and the only people answering doors are old couples and women.

"Sex," says Mickey. "S is for seduction, E is for eye contact, and X is for excitement."

"I'll remember that," I tell Mickey. I wonder when's the last time he had his ticket punched, if he's had sex with his ex-wife since moving into her basement. He's probably so worn out from having sex with customers, he has nothing left to give.

"Mickey, I have to pee." I've been holding it for a while, hoping the urge might go away.

"We'll go back to the woods. You can pee there."

"What about toilet paper? Do you have any toilet paper?"

"No. See, I don't have that problem, I don't need toilet paper. Most times, I tell the girls to use leaves, but the leaves are wet, so . . . " He pulls his cigarettes out of his pocket and lights one. The heavy rain has stopped. It's drizzling.

"Alright, then the woods it is."

I think of my brother. He's mentioned the Army is desperately short on equipment. Don't be fooled by the TV footage. Most Canadians walk around in a media-induced haze. Those Hummers you see us cruising around in? They belong to the Americans, we had to borrow them because we didn't have enough wheeled transport of our own. We didn't even have proper training.

We track back to the woods. We pass the houses of yes's, no's and maybe's. I notice the wind is picking up. A *For Sale* sign in front of a brick two-story house rattles back and forth on its hinges. I am unbelievably cold.

When we reach the woods, I tell Mickey I'll be back in a couple of minutes. I walk through the straggle of trees. There's an apartment building on my right-hand side. If someone looked out of their window, they might have a laugh, but who cares? My bladder is about to topple over. I unbutton my dress pants, pull them down along with my underwear, and squat over the wet leaves. A tree shudders above me, splattering rain onto my lower back. I close my eyes. I hear a trickle on the wet leaves. A trickle that starts and stops. It gathers momentum. Finally I stand up, pull my pants up, savor the small prize of relief.

Mickey is standing at the edge of the woods, jotting something down with a short pencil attached by a string to his clipboard.

"We have to do Beechville Estates," he says.

"Beechville Estates?"

"Yeah, it's this really nice area, used to be black people living there, but they kicked 'em all out and fixed it up."

"Kicked them out?"

"Well, most of them. There might be one or two left."

"Which way to Beechville Estates?"

"We're not goin' there right now," Mickey sighs. "You shoulda known that. We gotta finish the street we're on. In this business, you gotta be organized. It's what I've been tryin' to tell ya. You gotta have a plan."

He stops walking and turns to face me. "The way Tim explains it, it's like buyin' groceries. You enter this Superstore, big as a football field. Now some people have a list . . . "

"OK, Mickey! I scream. "I get it! I get it, already!"

"That's good," he says, "I'm just tryin' to help ya. It ain't easy. It ain't easy to get organized, take control and remain in control, know what you're selling."

I start to recognize familiar landmarks. The *For Sale* sign. A gray two-story with a yard consisting of small stones. We keep walking. I smell wood smoke. To be sitting in front of a fire, now, peeling off my wet socks. A woman in a bright yellow raincoat, standing on her front lawn, waves in our direction. I wave back automatically. A dog is squatting in the driveway. "Vanessa!" the woman calls. It's the woman who doesn't get into Halifax often.

We're approaching a two-story with a small flagpole jutting out from the porch. The flag depicts a snowman in a black hat. A carrot for a nose. Mickey rings the doorbell.

A woman whose face is crosshatched with heavy wrinkles, opens the door. She must be in her seventies. Her hair is dyed red, the gray roots showing. It reminds me of a rusty SOS pad.

"Oh you poor things," she says. "Whatcha doin' out on a day like this? Come in, come in."

The house smells of air freshener. A long striped rug leads down the hallway to the kitchen. I can make out a shelf filled with canisters, a window dripping with various stained glass ornaments.

A man leaning on a cane emerges from a room covered with avocado green carpet. "What's goin' on?" he says irritably.

"I found these fellas on the doorstep," the woman says.

"Whatcha sellin'?"

Mickey takes a book of coupons from his clipboard, "Sir, I'm here on behalf of Taylor/Ford to offer you a free oil change."

"Ross don't drive anymore," says the woman, "but we gotta son, Robert, and he drives. Sweet Jesus, does he drive. You wouldn't believe all the drivin' he does, drives from the South Shore to Dartmouth every morning, works all day at that chocolate factory, then drives back, sometimes I worry . . . ya know the roads aren't that good, and his wife . . . "

"Audrey, shut your pie-hole!" her husband shouts.

"Sounds like your son could use these coupons," says Mickey, "He'll save big bucks. It would make a great Christmas gift."

"Sure!" says the woman, brightly. "We'll take it."

"No, we won't!" says the man.

"Well, *I'm* going to take it. It's my money, my pension. It's not everyday someone comes to the door with something nice I can put in Robert's stocking."

"It's not Christmas," the man says furiously. "It's not even November."

"It saves me from going down to the mall."

"It saves you from nothing."

"Ross, where's my purse?" she screams.

"How should I know?" Ross says, smirking at us.

Audrey shakes her head. "The ol' bugger's gone and hid my purse. He did the same thing last week. Could you fellas come back later?"

"No problem!" says Mickey. "When?"

"Anytime. Just give me a while to find where he hid it."

"Sure thing. Thanks, Audrey." Mickey bows, bending at the waist. The pencil attached to a string, flies from his clipboard, swinging out like a bungee jumper.

"See what I told you about the maybe's being the most valuable?"

I realize now, if I had held on for another house, I could have used Audrey's bathroom.

At the next house, I ring the doorbell. A girl, about eight years old, flings the door open. Her pink sweatshirt is appliquéd with a smiling turtle and yellow flowers.

"Watch this!" she says, pushing with her hands at either side of the doorframe. She lifts a bare foot and places it against the wood, under her hand. She attaches another foot to the opposite side and edges her way up the doorframe like a spider.

"Is your mother home?" Mickey says.

The girl looks down at him from her elevated position. "Maybe she is, maybe she isn't."

"Look, kid, get your mother," says Mickey. "If you don't, I'll tell Santa."

*It's not even November,* I think to myself.

"I'll tell Santa on you. On you, on you, on you," the girl sings from above.

"Who's that, Chelsea?"

"It's an ugly man and his wife," shrieks the girl. She leaps onto the welcome mat and dances around. "Wanna see my pet rats? I got two pet rats."

"Male or female?" I ask. Mickey looks at me. Disgust is written all over his face.

"Two females. I wanted a boy and a girl but daddy said no 'cause then they'd make babies and we'd have a million babies. I had a chameleon but it died. It was only this big," she says, holding up her pinky finger.

"Chelsea, that's enough!" A woman with black hair cropped close to her head yanks Chelsea to one side. "May I help you?" she says.

"Don't worry, I ain't here sellin' religion," Mickey asserts.

"We happen to be a religious family."

"Oh," says Mickey, caught off guard. "Well, in that case, you don't gotta buy it. My name is Mickey, and I'm here on behalf of Taylor/Ford . . . "

The woman points to a No Solicitors sticker on the front door. "Can't you people read?"

"I can read!" Chelsea screams. She jumps up and down, full of joy. "I can read!"

"Yes you can," says her mother. "But apparently these people can't."

"Oh, I can read," says Mickey. "But you see, I read the sign after I rang the doorbell, and I didn't think it would be polite to run away."

"Well, you can run away now," says the woman. "Run, run, off you go." I turn and walk down the steps.

"Oh my God," I say to Mickey.

"Well, you get all kinds in this business. You can't let it getcha down."

How can you *not* let it get you down, I wonder. I doubt Tim ever had to put up with women telling him, "run, run, off you go". All that stuff about opportunity for advancement is probably a load of crap. "So how do you advance in this company?" I ask Mickey.

"That's a good question. I was wondering when you'd start to ask questions. First you gotta stick it out for a year and show a level of competence."

"How do they measure your level of competence?"

"By how much you sell and other stuff, you gotta be a team player. If you show a level of competence, then you advance to the next stage, training people."

"What happens after that?"

"First you gotta show a level of competence training people. That's where I'm at now."

"So if I quit, that's a strike against you?"

"Yup," says Mickey. "But don't worry. Not everybody is cut out for this business. It's a fact of life. The strong stay, the weak fade away."

It's raining again. The rain beats down like a form of punishment. I start to sing a song my grandfather sang. *Raindrops keep falling on my head. Dee dah dah dumdididdy dah dah dah* I sing.

Mickey looks totally impressed. "That's a really great attitude! You know, to be honest, I didn't think you were cut out for this business, but I've changed my mind. See, I've been in this business so long, I can read people, but every so often someone surprises me. You really surprised me, breaking into song like that. That's a good example of A.A."

"I'm nothing if not a songbird," I chirp. I feel a kind of euphoria. I'm above all this. I have options. I have an English degree. When I've had enough, I'll go home. I'll call a cab from somewhere, and ask the driver to stop at an instant teller machine. I'll withdraw my last twenty dollars. One thing for sure, I'm not getting back in that van.

Outside Tim's office, I signed a document, freeing the company of any liability regarding my safety. I was among seven other trainees. "It's just a formality," Tim assured us.

We had to write down our names, our next of kin. The man beside me removed his baseball cap and scratched his forehead. For Next of Kin, he printed. Mom. The others obediently signed their respective papers, so I did too, thinking *What could possibly happen?*

Now I wonder how I could have signed. What made me get into that van? If they had asked me to go to Afghanistan, would I have done that too? Maybe my brother is right — the average Canadian taxpayer doesn't ask questions. Has no clue that the "Canadian Battlegroup" is not a standard military formation, but more like the German Kampfgroup, a group of available support units. Not that I pay a lot of taxes. But, I could have died in that van, and no one, not one member of my family, would have received an iota of compensation.

Mickey and I approach a duplex with an ornamental cedar in front. The two sides are mirror images, like the butterflies I made as a kid, folding the paper in half, so the paint smudged symmetrically on either side. We climb the steps on the left and ring the doorbell. A woman with blonde hair piled on top of her head answers the door. "There's a sign," she says, pointing to the No Solicitors sticker on the mailbox.

"Well, first I rang the doorbell. Then I saw the sign . . . "

"Oh. Could you hold on for a moment? I have something on the stove."

"Sure," says Mickey.

The woman leaves the door slightly ajar and disappears.

"See how that works?" says Mickey.

"What works?"

"What I say about reading the sign after I ring the doorbell. That's the importance of observing. You can learn a lot from observing."

So far, I've observed this subdivision is a kind of no man's land. Nine times out of ten, the doors are opened by women. Most husbands come home between six and seven o'clock and the wives shy away from making any commitment regarding car dealership coupons. They are much more Pizza Sensation-coupon friendly.

The woman returns. I hear Mickey pontificating about the free oil change, but I'm not really listening. "Just a minute, I have to ask my husband."

"Her husband's home?" I say.

"Yeah, I can see him reading the paper."

The woman returns to the door. "I'm sorry, but my husband does all that for himself." She shuts the door.

"If her husband does all that for himself, then why couldn't he come to the door for himself?" Mickey says.

I wonder if we'll get a mirror-response from the other side of the duplex, but no one answers the door. Mickey draws a stick-duplex on his map. He marks an X and leaves the other side empty.

"Why don't you just write down the addresses?" I ask.

He pauses. "I can't read or write that good. See, I'm dyslexic. When I look at numbers or try to read words, they get all screwed up in my head. I see them in reverse. I was never good in school, except for art. I always got A's in art. While you were in the woods taking a leak, I drew this picture of you."

He flips up the map on his clipboard and shows me the paper beneath. It's amazing. I look like The French Lieutenant's Woman, with my hood up. Caught off guard. Hesitation diluted by fear.

"Mickey, that's incredible! Where did you learn to do that?"

"I learned by doing it. I draw every day."

"Mickey, you could do this for a living! You probably think I know nothing, but I went to university. I minored in Art History. I spent years looking at paintings and drawings. You could make a living from your art, you just need the right person to promote you."

"Yeah, well, it ain't that easy." He reaches into his coat pocket and pulls out his cigarettes. He tries to light one, but the rain and wind interfere.

I suggest we stand under the porch of the right-hand side of the duplex. No one's home, anyway. He can smoke his cigarette.

Mickey agrees. We walk back up the path, and Mickey stands facing the door and lights his cigarette. I reach for my thermos and pour a cup of coffee. It's lukewarm. I rinse it around my mouth and swallow. I pour another cup for Mickey. When he's finished his cigarette, he butts it out on the side of the porch and throws it over the side.

We approach an executive ranch with a beautiful yard, and a tall, slim woman with short salt and pepper hair answers the door.

"My name is Mickey, and I'm here on behalf of Taylor/ Ford . . . "

Then he starts to cough. "Excuse me," he says. He coughs again, turning away from the door. I stand there, watching. Fifteen seconds elapse, and he's still hacking.

The woman looks on helplessly. "Please come in!" she says. "I'll get you a glass of water." It doesn't appear as though Mickey has much choice. The woman takes hold of his arm, the sleeve of his wet baseball jacket. "Come in," she says to me.

I stand in the foyer while she guides Mickey down the hall, under a chandelier, and into a room.

"You come too," she calls.

I pad down the hallway and enter the living room. Mickey is sitting on a black leather reshaped sofa, holding a box of Kleenex. The woman is nowhere to be seen.

I sit down next to Mickey and check out the home entertainment system, a wide screen with video projection, surround sound, a DVD player. The coffee table is a sheet of smoky glass poised on three stainless steel legs. Everything in the room is reflective, slippery and ultra modem, ready to take off into another galaxy.

The woman returns with a glass of water. I pray Mickey has the decency not to try and ply her with coupons. Not after she's been so hospitable.

"Whatever you're selling, I'll buy it," the woman says. "It looks as though you're having a hard day."

Mickey looks stunned. "Well, we're promoting two companies. See, here's the coupons."

"How much are the coupons?" the woman asks.

"Twenty-four ninety-nine per booklet."

"Oh." She pauses for a split second. "I'll take one booklet. One sec." She walks out of the room, returning with a black eel-skin wallet. She takes out thirty dollars. "Here you go. Keep the change."

He takes the cash and stuffs it in his baseball jacket. "Ma'am, which coupons do you want, the Pizza Sensation coupons or the ones for Taylor/Ford?"

"The ones for Taylor/Ford, I guess."

"It's a great deal. You won't be sorry," says Mickey. He hands her the coupons.

"You know," says the woman, leading us to the door, "you should really see a doctor. That's a terrible cough. You could get pneumonia walking around in the rain like that. If I were you, I'd just go home, make a nice cup of lemon tea."

"I wish I could, Ma'am, but a man's gotta work."

"Well, I wish you two the best of luck in all your endeavors."

*Endeavors.* Is that some kind of a joke? "Thank you," I say.

"We got a hit," Mickey says. "Thank fuck. I'm gonna run out of cigarettes at two-thirty."

I look at my watch. How can it only be one o'clock? I want to die. I want to go home. At the same time, I feel bad about leaving Mickey. I don't have the heart to tell him — a woman's gotta go home.

"Mickey," I say, "why don't we go back to Audrey's? She must have found her purse by now."

"We can do that later. We should really finish this street."

"Mickey, I have to go to the bathroom. It could be messy. I don't want to use the woods again. I'm sure Audrey will let me use her bathroom."

"OK." He scribbles on his map and we walk back the way we came. Audrey answers the door.

"Ya fellas back? Time sure flies. Come in, come in. Here, let me take your coats. Take your shoes off. I haven't found my purse yet. See, Coral called. My sister. She just had a hip operation."

We follow Audrey into the living room where her husband is sitting on a blue recliner watching television.

"You're back," he grumbles.

"I bet he hid it in the kitchen," Audrey says. "He figures that's the last place I'll look."

"Do you think I could use your washroom?" I ask.

"Of course, my lamb."

It's immaculate, like one in a hotel — cream coloured floor tiles, mint green walls, mint green hand towels with embroidered flowers, and a scalloped sink.

When I re-enter the living room, Mickey and Ross are watching TV. I sit down beside Mickey and stare at the screen. George Bush is talking about the attacks on Afghanistan. *"We will not relent in — waging this struggle for freedom and security for the American people,"* he says from a podium, the American flag behind him.

"He talks the same way you do," says Ross, addressing Mickey and myself.

I have no idea *what* he's talking about. I talk a certain a way, Mickey talks a certain way, but neither of us talks likes George Bush.

"Next, he'll bomb Iraq," says Ross. "After that, it'll be North Korea. Mark my words."

Audrey appears, walks across the carpet towards her husband, bends down and peers under the skirt of the blue recliner. "Ross, where'd ya put my purse?"

*"Freedom and fear are at war. The advance of human freedom — the great achievement of our time, and the great hope of every time — now depends on us."*

"Freedom," says Audrey's husband. "Use the word 'free,' and everyone jumps. Free oil change, dream of freedom, freedom holes."

"Freedom holes?" says Mickey, "What are freedom holes?"

"After George Bush drops a bomb, that's what he calls the craters."

"Ross gets everything wrong." Audrey says. "We were watching a comedy show last night, and a reporter who wasn't really a reporter, made a joke about the craters being freedom holes. The reporter was pretending to be in Afghanistan."

"My brother's in Afghanistan," I say.

Ross lights up. "Your brother's a soldier?"

"Yup."

"Ross fought in World War II, and then the Korean War," says Audrey. "Our daughter's in Korea."

"Your daughter's in the military?" I say.

"Lord, no," Aubrey says, "she tutors a bunch of Korean bigwigs in English."

"Wow!"

"They treat her like a princess," Aubrey says. "Pay her a big salary and give her a free apartment and all she has to do is talk to them. She buys all the clothes she wants. Not a care in the world."

"A person's gotta do what they gotta do," Mickey pipes up.

"All them missiles pointed at them across the DMZ," Ross grumbles.

*"Make no mistake. We will prevail,"* George Bush says, glaring at us across the screen.

"Hey, I think I can see a purse," I say.

It's in the fireplace under a bunch of artificial logs in an ornamental wrought iron holder.

# THE BLUE LOBSTER

THAT YEAR THE lobster fishermen hauled in traps blooming with fully mature blue lobsters. Everyone was baffled. There was much talk.

Everywhere the weather suddenly decided not to. Baggy clouds exploded with sunshine. The weather forecast was consistently completely off. People smelled the air suspiciously, as if it were slightly rancid hamburger meat. Hail the size of garden peas preempted rain. Rain preempted heavy snow.

"Vanessa," Erika told her dog who was frantically lapping up puddle juice, "I don't think that's very healthy."

She had read somewhere that it was a good idea to talk to your dog the same way you talked to humans. Otherwise they might suspect foul play. Vanessa stampeded through another puddle with a stick in her mouth. Her parents were both thoroughbred German shepherds, American champions — her father, Just Gus, and Mother, Morning Star of Vanelle. Erika explained this to people who made statements like, "God, does that ever look like a wolf!" or "That dog is better behaved than most children." Erika had paid a reputable breeder quite a chunk of money. It wasn't a case of animal elitism, but of fear. Erika loved dogs, and the thought of losing one to bone cancer or something else like that, was more than she could bear.

They were making tracks through the grounds of the museum, and had reached one of Vanessa's favourite topographical features: a large crater she circled obsessively like a finger the rim of wine glass. Erika leaned against a tree trunk and watched, then chipped away at a thin layer of ice with her boot. 'The Ice Man Melteth,' what a dumb idea that was!" she said to Vanessa, who was attracted by the tinselly sound. "The Ice Man Melteth" was an essay she'd written last semester for an English class. It was an in-depth analysis of Hickey's conversion in Eugene O'Neill's play.

*Let's not get too silly!* the professor scrawled on the cover page, a big black arrow aimed at her title. Since then, she couldn't think of a title without freezing up. "Call it 'Untitled'," suggested her husband Nick last week, "that's what I call most of my paintings, that or something numerical."

Nick was thirty-one now, a beautiful man with olive skin and eyes like the big brown buttons on a corduroy jacket. They'd met in a small prairie town at the Fine Arts campus where Nick was doing his MFA. Erika was enrolled in her second year of theatre studies. They'd each drifted down the same hallways, and strolled back and forth to the coffee machine that spewed out dark liquid without ejecting paper cups. They'd attended the same sad theatre productions and the parties afterwards when the actors emerged from their dressing rooms wearing towels that barely covered their thighs and danced around the room, singing *Fame, I'm gonna live forever . . .*

After one of these parties, Erika made a detour and found herself in front of a door that said, *Painting Studio*. She knew this was where Nick created his large, colour-field paintings. Once, she'd peeped in when a girl was staring at two of his panels, one a buttery yellow, the other, a combination of blues.

"That one's a field of wheat, right?" the girl said, "and that one's supposed to represent the sky?" She was wearing tight blue jeans with pink leg warmers.

"I suppose," Erika heard Nick say sarcastically.

"You should know," said the girl. "You're the one who made them."

Nick came from Nova Scotia. That much Erika knew. She'd heard other things, though. That he did a striptease for one of his professors. That he removed women's tampons with his teeth and drank their blood. Apparently, he was straight; apparently, he was gay, a slut, a chick-magnet; apparently, he'd done it with animals. People on the prairies had hyperbolic imaginations.

The door of his studio was closed. Usually, she could smell turpentine, hear the march of footsteps or strains of Bob Dylan. *It's all over now. Baby Blue.* She took her knapsack off and searched one of the pockets until she found a bottle of liquid paper. With the small brush, she blotted out an O and two I's, so the plaque on his door read *Panting Stud*. Then she wondered why she did it. She followed some straggling theatre students, high on themselves, shimmying down the hallway into the dark night.

The next morning, in acting class, their professor said, "Ok, people, become a bird, any bird, just pick a bird and *work with it*." The class took place in a room with three walls of mirrors and a dance bar running all the way around. Erika felt herself getting lighter. Already, she was skittery from three cigarettes and a thermos of coffee purchased at the 7-Eleven. The coffee from the machine in the hallway, even if it did decide to dispense a cup, tasted more like chicken soup.

"The way to get around it," a visual arts professor once explained to her, standing in front of the coffee machine, "is to stop regarding it as coffee altogether." The professor was a conceptual cartoonist, tall, thin, and slightly balding. "If you let go of the coffee-expectation," he said, "suddenly that black liquid becomes tolerable, it becomes nothing more than what it is."

"Don't brood on your choice of bird," shouted the acting professor. He always left the door open, so students from other disciplines could look in at them like they belonged to another planet. Suddenly, Erika was a parrot. She cocked her small head and looked in the mirror, amazed at the transformation. Not only was she a parrot, but a very pretty parrot — blue and red with a streak of yellow. Basically all your primary colours. She flew around the room. Then through a rain forest, slicks of green everywhere sieving the sunlight. Flying down, it was possible to see a jaguar relaxing in the dark aisle of a tree's roots. Now a voice. *Come on, people, you can do better than that. Don't think about becoming a bird. It's like sex, ya don't think about it, ya just do it.*

"It's like sex," Erika squawked with her parrot voice, "it's like sex, it's like sex." The professor rolled his eyes. What do I care, she thought. What's he gonna do? Fail a parrot? She flew around the room some more until the professor told them all to stop.

"Now," he said, "pick an animal, any animal, and work with it." She missed the rain forest already and decided to come back as a nine-banded armadillo. It was much slower going, however. Something smelled rotten, completely fetid, but she moved on. A black army boot impeded her progress.

"Hello," it said, "hello down there." She looked up. It was Nick. "Yes?" she said.

"Jack Pratt said he saw you last night fucking around with the sign on my door." Erika looked down. She felt frightened and curled up into a tiny ball. A minute later, she denied responsibility for the act of terrorism, and suggested that perhaps Jack Pratt was mentally ill and hallucinating. Nick, who hated nearly everyone he'd met at the Fine Arts Campus, found Erika's dislike for Jack Pratt attractive. He asked her out for dinner.

That evening, they walked downtown to a Vietnamese restaurant Nick said reminded him of an opium den. The restaurant was long and narrow and so dimly lit, they could barely see their food. They sat in a booth with plush upholstery and watched smoke billowing out of the kitchen. Over spring rolls Nick talked about his major thesis advisor, a woman called Barb Kindopp. Barb Kindopp's work involved writing angry pieces of text on photographs. First of all, Nick complained, he didn't even get to pick his thesis advisor. She was just assigned to him. But the problems really started when Barb wanted him to experiment more. She thought Nick should forget about painting for a while and begin to collage photographs onto pieces of fiberglass.

"My BFA was about experimentation," Nick said, squirting plum sauce over a spring roll, "I took film classes, photography,

I have a minor in art history. I mean, fuck, an MFA is no time to figure out what medium you want to work in."

After the spring rolls, they ordered charbroiled chicken vermicelli and more beer. Erika explained that although she was doing OK in her acting classes, she was actually getting better marks in her dramatic literature and theatre history classes. Then, one day, her acting professor asked everyone to invent a character and write three pages from the character's point of view. When he returned the papers, a week later, he said, "Erika, have you ever considered becoming a playwright or just a writer? Not only is this imaginative and well-written, but it revealed amazing things about the character, unbeknownst to the character herself." Now she was confused. Maybe she should switch to English. She'd always wanted to act, but her acting professor said she had trouble letting go of her inhibitions.

"Yeah, well," said Nick, "I think there's a little too much letting go around that department."

By February, she and Nick had moved in together, or rather, she moved a cardboard box full of clothes into Nick's one-bedroom apartment, a block away from the Fine Arts campus. The living room contained a chair, a table with one bad leg, a garbage bag full of empty beer bottles and an ashtray on the windowsill. The bedroom had an old mattress on the floor.

"The balcony will be nice when it gets warmer," said Nick, "we'll sit out there and drink copious amounts of alcohol."

"But we only have one chair," said Erika.

"We'll steal more from the Fine Arts campus."

The thing Erika loved most about Nick's apartment was its lack of television and telephone, the way not having the basic trappings annoyed other people, especially her conservative family. "What do you mean, you don't have a phone?" said Erika's sister as if she'd stepped on a thumbtack on the floor of Erika's existence. "I think that's totally ignorant."

"Oh, I know," said Nick. "People think you're weird if you don't own a TV, but they think you're *nuts* if you're phoneless." Nick didn't care about a phone, but he would speak nostalgically about TV, how much he missed both TV and the ocean: "I used to love watching TV, the news, old movies, nature shows, I think it's because I'm primarily a visual person. God, I miss the ocean. I grew up in the country, in front of the longest white sand beach in Nova Scotia. Our family had a lamb, Larry the Lamb, ducks, chickens, even two pet crows, Pete and Repeat. I hate this fucking place, I don't know how people can live here, it's so cold and claustrophobic."

"Claustrophobic?" said Erika. On the prairies, you can see forever. There's nothing but space."

"That precisely why it's so claustrophobic," Nick said. "The horizon line's like a dead heartbeat on a heartbeat monitor. And there's no humidity. When I graduate in the spring, I'm gonna roll up my canvases, pack up my guitar and hightail it back to Nova Scotia.

"What about me?" asked Erika. "What about the balcony in the spring?" She felt like singing, *I've grown accustomed to your face.*

In the evenings, while Nick worked in his studio, making paintings for his graduating exhibition, Erika strode around their vacant living room and recited lines for an upcoming audition. She was trying out for the lead female role in play called *The Captive.* It was by a growing-more-famous-everyday New York playwright, their dramatic literature professor informed them. It was on the cutting edge. It involved a love hexagon or two love triangles attached at the base, as the professor explained, drawing a colourful diagram on the whiteboard. After she worked on her lines, she walked the block to Nick's studio. They had a few drinks while Nick strummed his guitar. After that, they walked several blocks to the bar at the Plains Hotel, a bar that attracted hippies, artists, hippy-artists, accountants in bright Hawaiian shirts, bikers dipped in black leather like the ice cream cones, swirled and dunked in chocolate, a block away at the Dairy Queen. Nick and Erika collapsed into long booths with other people, talking, drinking, smoking, spilling popcorn on the carpet until the bartender who was a local photographer, closed the place up.

Erika's parents didn't approve of Nick, nor Erika for that matter. Erika's father, a structural engineer, hoped Erika would become a mechanical engineer like her sister. If not an engineer then something remotely practical, a scientific researcher or computer programmer. Erika's mother taught violin at the Conservatory of Music and played with the symphony orchestra. Although she thought Erika's decision to study acting was absurd, what really plagued her was the fact Erika had quit studying the violin. She had started Erika when she was three years old and had coached and nurtured her musically for years, along with numerous other teachers. Over the years, Erika placed first in music festivals and in the summer, flew to New York and Boston to attend prestigious music camps and master classes. Then, at the age of sixteen, she wrote her family a long letter, explaining that she wanted to quit, because the demands of constant practising, and the long hours of solitary confinement didn't suit her character.

She would never be a concert violinist and she didn't want to spend her life playing second violin in a third-rate orchestra. Or tenth violin in a first rate orchestra. Besides she drank too much coffee — the caffeine was affecting the fluidity of her bow-work.

Her mother and her music teachers were mortified. *How can you just throw everything away?* But, I never chose to make the violin the sole focus of my life, Erika argued. You chose for me. Her father had convinced her mother to look on the bright side, as the life of a musician was unpredictable at best, and perhaps she'd be better off becoming an engineer and later in life, as she was bound to return to music, playing in chamber groups.

In the end, what they couldn't forgive was the giving-up-violin/wanting-to-study-theatre combo. They saw Nick as just an extension of the combo, like a large Coke or a side of fries. Perhaps out of curiosity, they invited The Side of Fries over for dinner, along with a young couple new to the community and another couple they had known for years. Nick dreaded the event. He was in agony for days, wondering what he should wear, whether he had socks that matched. All his pants were splattered with paint, he said.

"Nick, you're not getting out of it," Erika said. "We have to go."

In the living room, before the meal, he sat on the couch, his right leg jiggling. In acting, this was called 'leaking energy.' He gazed at the porcelain busts of Beethoven and Brahms on the mantelpiece, the reading lamp that looked a little too modern, angling down like an ostrich. Then Erika offered to give him a tour of the house. She showed him her childhood bedroom with its hardwood floors and sky blue walls. Her bookshelf was filled with trinkets, a pewter container filled with potpourri now smelling of nothing, a theatrical mask with a long beak. They sat on Erika's old bed. Nick looked shell-shocked. "This is too weird," he said.

"What did you expect?" she said.

Erika's mother called from downstairs that supper was ready. They walked back down to the dining room, where a roast beef piped hot steam over the guests' heads. Erika's father was pouring wine. Then he started carving up the roast. Nick sat next to Erika's mother at the end of the table. Erika sat at the other end next to her father.

After drinking two glasses of red wine and outlining his manpower problems, Erika's father, flushed in the face, started to dwell on Erika's decision to study acting.

"You, see," he said, "when Erika was young, she taped posters of famous actors to the wall above her bed. Not *real* actors like Peter O'Toole or Jayne Mansfield, but characters like the Bionic Woman, what was her name?" Erika's mother gave her husband *the look,* as if to say now is not the time.

"Lindsey Wagner," Erika said, her voice steely.

"Lindsey Wagner," her father repeated. "And John Travolta. And, what's her name? The woman hugging John Travolta?"

"Olivia Newton John," Erika sighed.

"Olivia *Newt'n* John," her father repeated in a loud voice, conjuring up in the minds around him images of a salamander with long eyelashes and bright red lipstick.

"Dad, say the name Isaac Newton," Erika said.

"Isaac Newton, now that was a man!" said Erika's father.

"When you say Isaac Newton, you say 'Newton' properly," said Erika. "Like *Fig Newtons.* When you say "Olivia Newton

John, you say Olivia *Newt'n* John. Not that I'm a big fan of Olivia Newton John."

"Formulated the law of gravitation, optical observations on the nature of light, by the time he was twenty-three. *Twenty three*," he said, speaking to Erika directly. In case she missed the subtext, he added, "a year younger than yourself."

"I thought Olivia Newton John was a singer, not an actress," said the paunchy colleague of Erika's father.

"You know how things go these days," said his wife. "They're often interchangeable."

"She acted in that movie *Grease*," said Erika's mother. "With John Travolta. Now, I think about it, we haven't heard much of them since."

Erika looked over at Nick, who seemed to be enjoying himself, and back to her father. "You're fifty-four,"she said, "and I don't see you making any optical observations."

"Don't upset your father, Erika," her mother said. "Remember his blood pressure."

"He has more than high blood pressure," Erika said, rolling her eyes. The man belonging to the young couple, sitting opposite Erika, laughed, his eyes twinkling. His wife sitting beside him gave him the elbow.

"You see," said Erika's father to the guests, "Erika thinks she's special. It's not enough to settle down and study quantum mechanics, like her sister. She wants to be a star. To see herself on posters. To be in the public eye."

"Right now, I'm reading *The Unbearable Lightness of Being* by Milan Kundera," the man belonging to the young couple said. "Has anyone read it?"

"Yes!" said Erika's mother. Her enthusiasm was directed as much towards a change in subject as towards the book just mentioned. "I saw the movie with Juliette Binoche and Daniel Day Lewis, and then I bought the book. Erika recommended it. It's even better than the movie."

"That's often the case," said the woman belonging to the couple Erika's parents had known for years.

"Anyway," said the young man, "in the book, Kundera says people can be divided into four categories, according to the eyes they crave. The ones in the first category crave the anonymous eyes of the public. Like performers and actors. The ones in the second category live for the eyes of people they know, like people in the community. The ones in the third category live for the eyes of the person they love. Kundera believes that people in this category and the first category are in the most danger, because if something happens to the loved one or if an actor loses his audience, they feel they have nothing left to live for."

"That's fascinating,' said Nick, "Which category would you say you belong to?"

"I'd say the third category. I live for the eyes of my wife."

"That's nice, dear," said his wife, beaming.

"It also puts you in grave danger," said the young man, nudging her.

"What's the fourth category?" said Erika

"The fourth category . . . Geez, I forget," said the young man. "I should remember. I just read it last night."

"I have the book!" chirped Erika's mother. "Do you think you could find the passage?"

"Sure," said the young man. "I finished chapter twenty-six of Part Six last night and they're short chapters.

Erika's mother ran off to fetch the book.

"Our acting teacher says people can be divided into four categories: earth, air, water and fire," said Erika.

"See?" said Erika's father, throwing up his hands. "This is what they teach her in the Theatre Department."

"It does seem a bit reductive," said the young man's wife.

"It is reductive," said Erika, "but it makes sense in terms of theatre. If you think of A Streetcar called Desire, Blanche is air, Stella is earth, Stanley is fire and — "

"Did you hear about that painting, Voice of Fire?" interrupted the paunchy friend of Erika's father. "It's made up of three stripes. Some gallery in Ottawa bought it for two million dollars."

Erika knew where this conversation going. It was a hot topic, these days. At least three times a week, at the bar, Nick ended up in a vicious argument, defending the National Gallery's purchase of the Barnett Newman painting.

"Yup," said Erika's father. "Two million dollars for a red stripe sandwiched in between two blue stripes. A nice Van Gogh, I could understand. But a painting with three stripes? A bucket of blue paint, a bucket of red paint, I could've done the same thing."

"Then, why didn't you?" said Nick.

"Because painting such a stupid painting wouldn't occur to me, even if I was an artist," Erika's father said.

Erika saw Nick's jaw muscles tensing up. "Sometimes," said Nick very slowly, "doing something that stupid, requires a certain amount of intelligence."

Erika's father guffawed. He turned to his paunchy friend for support. "I believe this young man is questioning my intelligence."

"No, I'm not," said Nick with irritation. "I'm just saying artists have to have a certain grain of stupidity, a grain of not taking certain things for granted, a grain of remaining transfixed by an object or scene for a very long time. This grain of stupidity considered from another angle, might be regarded as a form of intelligence. That's all I'm saying."

You may as well be talking to a brick wall, Erika thought. You're talking to a man whose life revolves around production kick off schedules and what he calls manpower/manhour situations. Earlier, when she went upstairs to the bathroom, she'd wandered into her father's study. There was an unfinished letter on his desk. It was about his latest contract. She started reading. *Drawing revisions,* her father had written, *resulted in scope increase that added approximately 40,000 manhours at a point in time when due to lack of schedule float every activity was on the critical path.* Could she really be the daughter of a man who wrote sentences like that?

Erika's mother came back, waving *The Unbearable Lightness of Being.* Saved by a Czech novelist, Erika thought to herself. Her mother handed the book to the young man who flipped through it, while Erika's mother offered the guests more roast beef, asparagus and potatoes.

"Ok," said the young man. "I've found it. He says the first category longs for an infinite number of anonymous eyes, like the German singer and American actress in the book. Those in the second category need to be looked at by many known eyes. He claims these people are the tireless hosts of cocktail parties and dinners."

"That's you guys," said Erika, addressing her parents.

"The third category," said the young man, "consists of people who need to be constantly before the eyes of the person they love. Like Tereza and Tomas in the novel. The fourth category is the rarest. They live in the imaginary eyes of those who are not present. Perhaps an absent lover or role model. Kundera says they are the dreamers."

"The imaginary eyes of those who are not present?" said Erika's father. "What kind of bafflegab is that?"

After being released from the dinner party, Nick and Erika went to the bar. Nick said her parents were Philistines. They had a bitter argument because Erika realized it was one thing to find fault with one's own family, but quite another to hear them trashed by an outsider. She thought of Nick and herself like a colour-field painting, two stripes of blue divided by the red of her parents. The red had to be eliminated somehow.

"Nick," she said that night, "let's get married. I may have had five gin and tonics, but I'm serious."

"Just a small ceremony," she said. "Fuck my parents. We can invite some friends from the Fine Arts campus."

"Why not?" said Nick. "Then we'll hightail it back to Nova Scotia. Hey, why not get married there?"

The day Nick finished his thesis defense, which his examiners said he passed with "flying colours," he bought a second-hand car. They filled the trunk with his rolled up canvasses, two suitcases full of clothes, and made their way to Nova Scotia.

While they were driving, Nick chain-smoked and reminisced about his thesis defense. He had hung his colour-field paintings in a room in the local gallery. They were so large that three colour-field triptychs took up an entire wall. Nine people altogether, eight professors from the Visual Arts department and an external examiner, sat in a semi-circle surrounded by his paintings, and asked him questions. He reminded Erika that 95 percent of recent graduate students in Visual Arts had barely passed their thesis defense.

"Yeah, yeah," said Erika, popping a stick of peppermint gum in her mouth.

The external examiner had asked him whether he believed art should be political. Nick had argued everything a person creates is political by virtue of its existence in a political world. All creations have a political residue, he explained, tortured by bad gas brought on by a chicken salad sandwich he'd eaten in the cafeteria downstairs. But, no, he said, he didn't believe artists should be motivated by a political agenda per se, that's what voting, protests and revolutions were about. He gestured dramatically with his right hand.

"Keep both hands on the steering wheel," Erika said. "That guy in front of us has Ontario plates. There's no telling what could happen." The windows were down, and whole sections of her hair moved around her face like the arms of an octopus.

"Alright," said Nick, "So then Barb Kindopp asked me how I would respond to the accusation that my paintings were macho, that they belonged to a patriarchal tradition of painting."

"I bet you didn't see that one coming," laughed Erika.

"No kidding. So I said very calmly that, no, my paintings aren't about any swashbuckling facture, they're about process, a slow methodical building up . . . "

"Swashbuckling facture?" Erika interrupted. "What the hell is that?"

"I made it up," said Nick. "Swashbuckling like a pirate brandishing a paintbrush instead of a sword, and facture, as in manufacture. You should have seen their faces when I came up with that one! They looked as if they'd missed some boat along the way. After it was over, and everyone was congratulating me, Reed Addington, you know, the conceptual cartoonist, shook my hand and asked, 'How long have you been sitting on that one?'"

"'What one?' I asked," said Nick, throwing up his hands to dramatize the innocence of his query.

"Nick, keep both hands on the wheel," said Erika.

"'What one?' I asked," Nick repeated. "'Swashbuckling facture,' said Addington."

"Nick, do we have any scissors?"

Nick accused her of not listening to what he was saying. She said she *was* listening, but the wind had blown a chunk of hair into her mouth. It was now hopelessly attached to her chewing gum. To demonstrate her point, she spit the wad of gum out of her mouth and it swung like a bungee jumper from the side of her head.

"Oh, for fuck's sake," said Nick. He handed her his lit cigarette. *"Burn* it off. So, I told Addington I just made it up, right then and there, off the top of my head! He was incredulous, just incredulous. He whispered in my ear, 'Look, I'll buy ya two cases of beer if I can use that phrase in one of my cartoons.' 'No problem,' I told him. 'Go for it!' So we shook hands, sealed the deal."

Erika, not about to burn her hair, dragged on Nick's cigarette. "Two cases of beer? That's pretty cheap for someone's intellectual property."

"I might have an exacto knife in the trunk, in one those boxes with the paint brushes," Nick said.

Life didn't look too bad. Erika had applied and been accepted at a university in Halifax, where she would leave Theatre studies behind and take up with English literature. Perhaps acting wasn't the most practical thing after all. Future opportunities amounted to — if she was lucky — weaseling three roles a year from the local theatre company or working at community centers that arranged every summer for twenty rambunctious kids to be taken off their mothers' hands in the name of acting classes.

In the end, what got to her was the illusion of the fourth wall — getting on stage and pretending there's an invisible wall between you and the audience, and that nobody is actually out there watching you. And the audience partaking in a similar contract — pretending that you're not pretending every movement you make has been choreographed for their presence. Sitting there, night after night, in well-worn crimson snap-up seats, watching university productions, or during a trip to see productions in New York, her disbelief never left her. It stayed, like a dog, devoted to something that exceeds its own consciousness.

So, for the first time, she took out student loans, and mortgaged her future, but what the hell? She had even packed her violin, music stand and sheet music. In motel rooms along the way, she set up her music stand, rosined up her bow and practiced, while Nick drank beer and listened in amazement.

"I had no idea you could play like that!" he said.

"What are you talking about?" she said. "I'm rusty. I haven't practiced seriously in a long time."

When they finally arrived in Halifax, it was late afternoon. They checked into a bed and breakfast across from a small park. The sound of children playing must be one of the most beautiful sounds, Erika thought, opening the window — children unleashing their ecstasy, chasing each other in circles, like grown-ups do, but in more stylized, underhanded ways.

"Hello TV," said Nick, stroking the screen, "show me a cheetah, show me a school of fish." He opened a beer, flopped down on the bed, and turned on the TV. Erika decided to go in search of a cup of coffee. Nick always said coffee was her major problem. *You know what your problem is? You drink too much coffee. You wake in the morning and make yourself a pot of coffee, then you go out and wander around all day from coffee shop to coffee shop. Then you come home with a buzz-on, completely freaked out, like something out of an Edvard Munch painting. Then you complain you can't sleep. What a shock! You need to drink more water and less coffee.*

But, she loved coffee. She loved the smooth take-off — *May I have a coffee, please* — and the shaky landing, her thoughts crawling all over each other. Before the audition for *The Captive*, she'd knocked back two espressos at *Certainly Cinnamon*. She felt nervous, but terribly alert. She stood in the room with three walls of mirrors, the acting teacher and the director sitting before her like a two-man jury. After reciting a batch of lines, the acting teacher thrust out his hand. The director threw down his spiral notebook and informed her she'd just thrown away one of the most poignant lines in the play. Which line, Erika wanted to know. *We were the perfect communist couple.* He told her to keep in mind that this was the voice of an Eastern European woman in excruciating pain. Right now, she was speaking so fast, her character sounded high on crack cocaine. He told her to take it from the top, from *the lobster*.

*The lobster lies a predicate to its claw*
*like the regime that capsized our lives.*
*Adam, I needed release. For years, I walked the streets like a*
*cut-out,*
*wondering if you were still wearing the same shoes.*
*I realize now. I was a true subject, and we,*
*we were the perfect communist couple.*

"You still sound like a crack addict," the director complained. As far as Erika was concerned, so did a lot of American playwrights.

Nick said she'd have no problem finding a coffee shop. Because of all the universities, Halifax had tons of bars and coffee shops. She said she'd pick up a newspaper and check out the Classifieds. They should try and find an apartment as soon as possible.

She wandered up and down the streets, inhaling the salt air. She stopped at a seafood outlet where a blue lobster had ended up in a special tank. People were standing around talking and watching it swim around elastic free, as if it was in a pet store. They'd held a NAME OUR BLUE LOBSTER contest and, unbeknownst to the lobster itself, it had acquired the name Blue Bonnet.

Finally she bought a newspaper and found a coffee shop, where she ordered a double espresso. Distracted by the people around her, kids with their underwear showing, she put the Classifieds to one side and just drank her coffee. When she was finished, she ordered a take-out coffee and walked back to the hotel.

Nick was still lying in bed, the pillows propped up behind him, watching TV. There were three empty cans of beer on the bedside table. He said he wanted to visit Doug, an old friend, who'd played with him in a band called Slippery Chicken. Back then, Nick had shared studio space with a girl called Deirdre he later introduced to Doug. Doug and Deirdre been together ever since. Doug was like a brother to him, and Deirdre a sister.

"What does Doug do?" asked Erika.

"Not much," said Nick. "Paints the odd house, plays drums in a band. He's not a bad drummer, actually, but he's got the drummer complex."

"Drummer complex?"

"Wants to be a front man. Throws temper tantrums. Hates the fact he's stuck back there behind the guitars and lead singer."

"And Deirdre? What does she do?"

"Deirdre's the breadwinner. She teaches art classes. Whenever she has a show at some gallery, she sells a couple of her paintings to restaurants. She paints bowls of fruit and flowers. People buy her paintings because they're safe and conservative," Nick said bitterly. As they walked to the waterfront, Nick pointed out an old building, which jutted up suddenly. "That's where Doug and Deirdre live," he said. "It was a hotel originally, built at the turn of the century." Erika found the building visually disturbing. It tipped slightly to the left.

"It reminds me of the way the hat sits on the cat's head in Dr. Seuss," Erika said. She'd never seen a building like this on the prairies.

"Dr. Seuss must have based that Cat in a Hat on the Mad Hatter from Alice in Wonderland," Nick said. "D'you know where the expression 'mad as a hatter' comes from?"

"No," said Erika. "But I'm sure I will in a minute."

"A long time ago, beaver pelts in Canada were sent to England to be made into felt hats. They used toxic glue, which drove the people who made the hats crazy. So you see, there's this connection between Canadian beavers and that cat in Dr. Seuss." "How did you know that?" said Erika. "Everyone knows it," said Nick.

"*You always do that,*" she said, stomping her foot on the pavement. "You assume that just because you know something, everyone else does." Her calves ached from walking up and down hilly streets. "You sit around bars reeling off shit about sarcophaguses and scriptoriums, vellum and volutes, beaver pelts and *The Cat Came Back,* and everyone wonders did I miss something here, am I stupid?"

Nick was silent for the rest of the way. Once inside the building, they climbed an Escher-like dream of staircases. Doug, a pallid man with spiked black hair was waiting on a landing. "Hey, man," said Nick, embracing him. Doug kissed Erika on the cheek and led them into the apartment. "Most people just climb up the fire escape," said Doug. "It's easier."

Deirdre, a wide-eyed small girl with red hair and freckles, shrieked when Nick entered the kitchen. "*Oh my God!*"

The kitchen walls were covered with Deirdre's paintings, still life after still life on small blocks of wood. Every ledge exploded with flowers and fruit set-ups. "These days, I get a lot of pleasure out of looking and cooking," said Deirdre, "I'm becoming more domestic all the time." The kitchen table was covered with postcard size paintings of Halifax. Doug said he and Deirdre had been working on the paintings for a week. A big ship full of American tourists was expected to arrive the day after tomorrow. They planned to set up a table at the pier and sell the paintings for $25.00 apiece. "They really eat up this kind of shit," Doug said.

"Jesus Christ," said Nick. "Is the employment situation that bad?"

"Well, it's not great," Doug confessed. "This *is* the Maritimes."

Later Doug phoned David, a designer who lived below him. David, a forty-three year old man with a crooked smile and a cool haircut, climbed up the fire escape. He had a slow burning self-confidence and sat in a chair as if it were a throne, pouring out wine from the three bottles he produced from a leather satchel. He said he was planning to open up a bar downtown on Lower Water Street. It was a good location. Doug told him it was a dumb idea because Halifax already had the highest number of bars per capita in Canada, excluding Saint Johns, Newfoundland.

David nodded. He rubbed his right thigh clad in green denim. He admitted there were a lot of bars, but there was no place where people from the arts community could commune, have a few drinks and talk. He imagined a bar that was visually interesting, full of pillars and indoor trees. He would design it himself. He also wanted to put in a kitchen, so people could order food.

When they finished the three bottles of wine, David climbed down the fire escape to get more wine, brandy and whatever else. They were going to drink David out of house and home, Erika worried. Doug said Erika didn't know David. He had a fully stocked liquor cabinet for parties, in case guests showed up unexpectedly. David was the perfect host. He had a big apartment that used to be the reception area of the hotel. There was always booze and hors d'oeuvres on hand — cool things he popped in the oven and pulled out fifteen minutes later. You could say a lot of things about David. You could say David was a megalomaniac, an asshole, a womanizer, but you couldn't say David wasn't a great host. That's why people who called him names, ended up coming to his parties. They didn't want to miss out, and always felt better once they'd spilt wine on David's rugs, once they'd put a good dent in his liquor supply. After that, they hated David in a different way. They hated him gratefully. They felt grateful they could make fun of the latest sign he had designed, say the figures in his latest sculpture looked like Hiroshima victims. David was actually a good guy to know, Doug concluded.

That night. Nick and Erika announced they were going to get married, perhaps in the next couple of weeks. Driving across Canada, they'd talked about it a lot. They'd invent their own vows. Their wedding invitations would be homemade.

"Why bother?" said Doug. "A piece of paper doesn't keep two people together." "I know, why *I'm* getting married," said Nick, slightly drunk. "Because we need *stuff*. Wedding gifts. The staples of existence. Forks, plates, pots and pans, a TV."

"What about spoons and knives?' said Deirdre.

"Yeah, spoons," said Nick, "so when Doug comes over, he can bang on the pots."

"Anyway, I think this calls for a toast," Doug said. "It's too bad we don't have any champagne."

"I think I have some champagne," David sighed. "I'll be right back."

They got married in a campground surrounded by Nick's old friends — his childhood friends, and friends he had made during the four years he spent in art school in Halifax. They ended up renting the main floor of an old Victorian house the landlord had divided up into apartments. It had high ceilings, hardwood floors and free cable, which Nick considered a serious bonus. Erika was more enamoured of the fact it was partially furnished — a couch, a kitchen table and chairs. What was the good of free cable if there was nothing to watch it on, and there was no guarantee they'd get a couch as a wedding present. Through an inaccessible door, they could hear the man who lived in the basement, snoring and coughing, the murmur of a television. It was the only drawback. That, and the fact the kitchen was nestled up to the washroom. That, and the fact you had to walk through the kitchen to get the washroom, and walk through the washroom to get to the bedroom. Once they were settled in the apartment, Erika announced she wanted a dog. She told Nick the only thing this story was lacking was a dog. He said he wasn't aware this was a story, he thought it was called life.

# THE RESEMBLENCE BETWEEN A VIOLIN CASE AND A COCKROACH

ONE AFTERNOON, MR. O'Land drove his daughter who had just started kindergarten, to a house in which a man, slightly balding, had set up his own private practice. The man led them to a room. It had that high polish that comes with a lot of light and immaculate surfaces. The man beckoned her to sit down on a long oak table. She climbed up on a chair and sat down, her skirt flaring up and then settling like a green wreath around her bum.

The man announced that together they were going to do some special exercises designed to improve her breathing. That should prove fun, he added. The man walked the length of the room and returned with a candle. It was lit. He held it at arm's length, several feet from her face. He told her to inhale as deeply as possible. Then he told her to blow. "Keep blowing," he said. "That's right, keep blowing until the candle goes out."

The above — a small slice of her history — might account for what followed. A friend called me last night — she's studying literary theory in an English department somewhere across the border — and we talked about a story she was trying to analyze. "Have you ever noticed," she said, (I could picture her face curling up like the Kleenex I'd just blown my nose with and chucked into the fireplace) "the way most writers locate EVERYTHING in childhood?"

I hadn't noticed, but now I think about it, she may have a point. It could be a mechanism of some kind. In which case, Dear Reader, please forgive me. What happened to Clarissa could have started anywhere, with her lungs perhaps. But how do I historicize them? They were like anybody else's, supplied by two main trees divided into smaller and smaller branches as they progressed more deeply into her chest. She had asthma, so that at times her airways would narrow as if someone was choking her. Her chest made a symphony of noises, and people would press cold instruments there to listen.

Or it could have started that night at the symphony. Earlier, her mother had thrown three chicken pies in the oven. The family ate quickly (Clarissa burning her tongue) and flew upstairs to get dressed. When they trooped outdoors, the world had folded itself neatly into a crisp winter envelope. Clarissa looked around and breathed deeply. Crisp, she thought, crisp as hospital sheets without the hospital smell. A blue velvet dress fell from her shoulders down to her ankles. In her hand she held a matching evening bag, completely empty since Clarissa couldn't figure out what to put in it. Her father had suggested her asthma inhaler but on second thought, dropped it into his blazer pocket. She held the bag close to her as if it were a small velvet animal. Tonight, anything was possible, her world perfect, untracked-through. Her father took her hand and led her through the huge carpeted foyer of the symphony hall. He shook hands with people and introduced her. Their faces, big as spaghetti bowls, looked down on her. "Well, isn't *she* pretty?" they chimed.

"She's no dummy either," her father laughed. She looked up at him wondering whether he'd mention the tutor she needed since she spent most of the school year in a plastic oxygen tent. He didn't though.

When they found their seats, the lights dimmed and the orchestra made spitting sounds. She asked her mother what they were doing. Her mother said they were tuning up. After that, there came a hushing sound, and the instruments dropped quietly into themselves. The musicians, all in black, sat poised as if they expected the music to attack from one of the wings. But only a man walked in. Everyone clapped. He was holding a wand. First, he smiled at the audience — he was pleased everyone was clapping for him — and after that, he mounted a wooden stand so that everyone except the musicians had to stare at the back of his head. He flicked his wand around, drawing an invisible signature in the air.

The strings began licking at the silence, then some other instruments her father said were wind instruments seemed to push them up and carry them away. Clarissa, bored with certain parts of the program, focused on various members of the orchestra. A young woman with chocolate brown hair and a very pretty face sat second in the long squiggly line of violinists. Sometimes she turned a page and resumed playing effortlessly. How she managed to play, turn the pages, and keep an eye on the man with the wand — all at the same time — Clarissa had no idea. She stared at the woman and inhaled deeply. She held her breath for as long as possible, believing she had taken some part of the violinist into herself. At the same time as she stopped breathing, she closed her eyes and started praying, "God, please, make me like that woman playing the violin, *please* God, make me that beautiful, that good at something."

Then she began to study another musician — an ugly man fingering what her father had pointed out as a double bass. She blew out furiously. She believed if she stared at him and inhaled, she might possibly, in some way, imbibe him. Clarissa knew appearances weren't everything, but on a very base level, she valued them and wasn't about to take any chances: "Please, God, do not make me like that man." She eyed an old, frizzy haired blonde woman playing the flute. She blew out. She looked at a sallow man playing the oboe. She blew out, discharging the current of air she believed jam packed with the potential of contamination.

I cannot explain the rationale behind those she chose to incorporate and the others she took great pains to eliminate from her system. She was young, and I suppose Clarissa, like most kids her age, discriminated according to appearance, some indelible quality she found either captivating or repulsive and, of course, gender—she would rather die than end up looking like a man or growing whiskers. She had admired the chocolate violinist for her beauty, her ability to do several things at once, and the intensity that gathered the woman's features into a huddle.

The ritual, once in place, was extraordinarily time-consuming. Clarissa could not focus on anyone passively or with disinterest, as she believed the combination of looking and inhaling carried with it tremendous repercussions. She could not look at people without blowing one way or the other.

The ritual was temporarily interrupted when she forgot about it somehow or when she couldn't perform it without being completely conspicuous.

The symphony outing ended abruptly when Clarissa's father, noticing her strange breathing, decided she was on the brink of an asthma attack. He wouldn't hear otherwise, assuming she was lying in order to stay and hear the music. He took the inhaler out of his pocket and made her take two puffs. Then he tucked her under his arm like a briefcase, and carried her out to the car. As they drove home, he attributed the phantom asthma attack to the cigarette smoke in the foyer.

She now realized the ritual was not something she could explain away easily, let alone justify to anybody. If she told her father, he might think her silly and tell her to stop, since the breathing patterns mimicked so closely the breathing exercises she was supposed to do when an asthma attack loomed on the horizon. He'd be forever confused about whether she was genuinely in trouble, or just trying to exhale an undesirable person. No, she thought, best not to mention it to anyone.

Clarissa's breathing problems, like those of most asthmatics, were related to common allergies such as pollen, dust, mold, and dander and others that weren't so common. While she was in elementary school, her father took her each week to the Medical Clinic for allergy shots. The theory behind this "Immunotherapy" was by injecting small amounts of the allergen under the skin, her body would produce blocking or neutralizing antibodies that would prevent an allergic reaction. She lived in constant fear of each appointment. The nurse, Mrs. Brown, drove about twenty-four needles into Clarissa's back and arms, and Clarissa was expected to sit there calmly. At the beginning, her father sat beside her on a plastic chair. When the needles began, she begged him to distract her. "Daddy, tell me a story NOW, before another one goes in." "I don't know a story," he said. He looked uncomfortable, his face flushed. "Mrs. Brown," Clarissa pleaded, "do YOU know a story? You must know *one* story."

Then her mother, who could actually dream up a story, took over the role as allergy shot companion. She'd sit on the plastic chair, swaying back and forth, telling ghost stories, mystery stories, stories about her own life — the time during the war her family hid in a bomb shelter, how her parents used to feed her beer for breakfast, and curl her hair with hot tea. The problem was that the stories began to distract Mrs. Brown. She'd wait for the climax before giving the next needle, or jab a needle in too forcefully, expressing her disbelief or horror. And in the end, her mother just ran out of stories, or perhaps she simply grew tired of telling them. Maybe she just preferred to go shopping and pick Clarissa up after the whole ordeal was over.

The allergy shots eventually ended as well, though I'm not sure exactly why. But I do remember something. One evening, Clarissa found herself inexplicably depressed. She sat on a patterned carpet, rocking back and forth, and staring at a strange painting hanging over the fireplace. It seemed to be staring back at her. She exhaled deeply and turned her gaze elsewhere. The *Peter and the Wolf* record she usually enjoyed sounded awful. She lifted the needle off the record and stumbled into the kitchen where her father was peeling potatoes, and her mother was reading letters. Clarissa plunked herself down on a chair and waited for her parents to notice her. Her facial muscles sagged and her mouth opened part way, lacking the motivation to shut itself.

"What's wrong?" her mother finally asked. Tears drooled down Clarissa's face. Nothing was wrong, and yet she seemed to be drowning in a thick, tasteless gravy. Her father said she was experiencing melancholy. She'd never heard the word before, but she imagined holly, a prickly plant with red berries that appeared around Christmas time.

"Ahhh, melancholy, dark passion's somber lining," her father mused.

Clarissa told her parents how the kids at school after seeing her arms, called her a heroin addict, how they laughed at her needle marks, and jabbed their pencils into her skin in order to make more marks. Her father said that was a good way to get lead poisoning; her mother was more appalled by the fact that kids had actually heard of heroin. In any case, a month or two later, the allergy shots stopped.

Throughout elementary school, Clarissa switched schools almost as often as she switched asthma treatments. She left one school because paint fumes pervaded the hallways. She left another after six gerbils appeared in a wire cage at the back of the classroom. They were backdropped by a big poster of the Four Food Groups — grain, fruits and vegetables, protein, and dairy. The gerbils scuttled around blotting out the various depictions of grain products. Her departure from this school was precipitated by a violent asthma attack and by a huge fight between her parents and the teacher, who bore a marked resemblance to a rodent himself. Her parents insisted she should take precedence over the animals, while the teacher argued that the educational experience the gerbils had to offer should take precedence over

Clarissa. Her parents were grossly offended. Clarissa merely felt sorry for the gerbils, knowing the cruel fate they'd meet at the hands of her pencil- or geometry set-wielding classmates.

Another school, then. And with it, a bizarre inhaler with a small propeller inside. Several times a day, Clarissa inserted a small yellow capsule inside the center of the propeller. Twisting the inhaler punctured the capsule. A sharp inhalation on the mouth piece spun the propeller around and this, in turn, released a fine white powder into her lungs. Clarissa abhorred the whole process and avoided it as best she could. Lunchtime was the easiest, since the inhaler was packed in her lunchbox with a note that said, "Don't forget to take your inhaler." Her mother also scrawled another message on a hard-boiled egg. "Have a nice afternoon." Clarissa took the inhaler and removed the capsule that lay there like a yellow wish. She stuck it in her pocket, and when she was strolling home, she threw it down a grate or up a tree. If it was breezy, she crushed the capsule between her thumb and forefinger, and watched the wind snort it magically away.

∾

Clarissa died, of course. This happens to most heroines, especially when they're beautiful. At fifteen, beauty dawned on her as if whatever we call God had discovered her face, her limbs — everything for that matter — and raped them of their mediocrity. The transformation didn't phase Clarissa in the least, even though it seemed to take place, more or less from what we could tell, overnight. If anything, Clarissa considered her good looks like a parcel she had ordered long ago and always expected to arrive. Her parents and schoolmates, on the other hand, didn't know how to react. These schoolmates, who were actually little more than friendly acquaintances, feared invidious comparisons, while others, who hung around hoping Clarissa's beauty might reflect on them, soon rejected her when they learned she had no desire to be around boys (their windbreakers smelling of smoke, their spitballs and truncated speech), go to parties or anywhere for that matter besides the local library or the symphony hall. Clarissa, frankly, couldn't care either way. She preferred her own company. If she needed to blow out, there was no one to hinder her.

And yes, the blowing ritual was still an integral part of her daily existence, although it had changed over the years. She worried about the way her prayers were worded, if she'd forgotten to include something, if in the essence of a person she'd just inhaled, there was a sinister quality she hadn't noticed. What became important, then, was the amount of information God actually required. Did she have to spell everything out for him, or did he know her heart, what she would want incorporated or eliminated? In the end, she solved her problem by blowing out just about everybody.

Over the years, she'd amassed more rituals, some branching off from the blowing ritual and others that were in no way connected to it. She prayed for the well-being of her family, for an end to war, for all the animals in the world that were suffering or just having a bad day. Other rituals involved placing the books on her bookshelf according to which authors she thought would want to live beside each other; turning on the radio and rocking back and forth until she fell asleep at night. Rituals such as these. But where was I? Ah, yes, the subject of her beauty.

Her parents, deep down, suspected the transformation was not for the best. They gazed at her curiously over the dinner table. They spent long hours discussing what was to be done. As if anything could be done. They worried that she might join a modeling agency instead of attending a reputable university, or that she might become self-absorbed, vain, and indifferent, or might succumb to something worse — although they weren't sure what that something was, and couldn't for the life of them have named it.

One evening, Clarissa started reading a collection of stories called *The Penal Colony* by Franz Kafka. She flew through *The Judgment* and proceeded to *The Metamorphosis*. It begins with a young man waking up to find he's metamorphosed into a giant cockroach. As she read about Gregor coming to terms with his thoracic legs, she sighed and lay the book down on her floral bedspread. She sat for a moment, picking at the plastic threads by which a bedspread yeasts up in places like fresh bread and settles itself down again.

Then she picked up the book and continued reading to the point where Gregor's mother taps cautiously at the door and says, "Gregor, it's a quarter to seven, hadn't you a train to catch?" and onward, through Gregor's exit from his bedroom, his mother's falling on the floor among her outspread skirts.

Tears welled up in Clarissa's eyes, and she put down the book again. Good heavens, she thought. And then it suddenly occurred to her — perhaps her parents were suffering from the same shock, the same sense of loss as Gregor's parents. Granted there were differences. Clarissa had turned into a beauty whereas Gregor had turned into a cockroach. But the effect was the same.

Clarissa began to giggle. A minute ago she'd been crying. Now she rolled around on the mattress, laughing so hard her cheeks cramped. A tickle started in her throat, and she began to cough. Cough and laugh. Her parents and Gregor's parents. What a ridiculous parallel. The tickle in her throat wasn't abating, and she considered crossing the hall to the bathroom for a glass of water, or maybe to her parents' bedroom for a roll of breath mints.

Tap, tap — her mother knocked on the door. "Clarissa, are you alright?"

"Yes," Clarissa gasped, still choking.

"You're not having an asthma attack, are you?" her mother asked nervously.

"No," said Clarissa. "I'm fine." She wished she could become a cockroach for about five minutes. That would really give her parents something to worry about. Her asthma and her beauty would pale in comparison. "You don't sound fine." "Well, I am," said Clarissa. "I'm fine."

As quickly as beauty had possessed her body, the fantasy of becoming a cockroach took possession of her mind. It was halfway through October, and she'd agreed, quite unwillingly, to join several of her friend-acquaintances at a Hallowe'en dance. It might be bearable, she thought, if she were to dress up as a giant cockroach. That way she could build a blockade of sorts, between herself and others. She'd cocoon herself in a large hard shell in which, she'd have to learn, like Gregor in the story, to propel herself around without knocking into things. She wouldn't have to talk to anyone, and no one could talk to her. Maybe she could even install a light inside and take a book along.

She headed down to the public library to research cockroaches. The only two books were in the children's section, and they had beautiful illustrations that could help her to build her costume. The text, although skeletal and hardly scientific, was also helpful. She learned that each cockroach eye is made up of two thousand individual lenses. She learned that the brain of a cockroach is distributed through its abdomen as well as its head. She learned that cockroaches have small breathing holes along the side of their bodies and from there, a network of tubes branching out to carry oxygen to their innards.

She also learned that cockroaches can cause asthma attacks, since many people are allergic to them. Beside the word 'asthma,' she saw 'AZ-MA' in bold letters so that children unfamiliar with the word could learn how to pronounce it. She discovered that many cockroaches are transparent (TRANZ-PEAR-INT). For a moment, Clarissa considered going to the dance as a transparent, or at least as an opaque cockroach. It would be neat, she thought, to concoct a shell made of see-through fiberglass. She'd appear fuzzy, as people appear from inside an oxygen tent. Finally, however, she decided on a classic brown cockroach.

For a week and a half, Clarissa worked steadily at constructing the costume. She carved a mold out of Styrofoam and, with the help of her cousin Anita, who was a sculptor, she created a big brown fiberglass casing. Every day after school, Clarissa walked over to Anita's studio and fine-tuned her cockroach. She punched holes in the side for breathing space, and two more for her eyes. She lined the interior with blue velvet, and as an afterthought, installed a pouch for a book, a flashlight, and something to snack on. She attached hairy legs and antennae to the outside of the case. Sometimes she worried that the costume was becoming too freakish and ugly.

"Hell, no!" said Anita. "Take a look at my babies." Her sculptures were an ugly, crazy amalgam of steel, fiberglass, and glitter. Clarissa thought Anita was an amazing person. Often when Anita was down on her knees putting the finishing touches on something, Clarissa inhaled her. "God, please," she prayed, "make me as talented as Anita."

Clarissa worked relentlessly on the details, making the costume resemble, as much as possible, a magnified, five foot eight cockroach. The casing was wide and long, so that her actual legs and arms, decked out in brown fibrous material, appeared much shorter than they were.

The casing locked from the inside with metallic clasps. After she died, this created a lot of confusion. The clasps, along with the blue lining, led various people to believe she'd modeled the case on one that might hold a stringed instrument — a violin or a cello. Her mother, on the other hand, thought Clarissa had been inspired by a lunchbox, because the clasps were similar. "There was many a morning," she sighed, "when I'd throw in a good book in case she got bored during recess."

"That's ridiculous," someone (probably Clarissa's father) said, "just ridiculous." If the costume was modeled on a violin case, then everything might stem from that singular evening when Clarissa first laid eyes on the chocolate violinist. If it was based on her lunch box, then the chief irony is that she neglected to pack an inhaler, which might have saved her life. No one's really sure, though, because at one point Clarissa fell. She also had an asthma attack. If the asthma attack took place after the fall, which knocked her unconscious, the inhaler would have been of no use anyway, even if she had thought to pack it.

Clarissa's cousin, Anita, had observed that Clarissa's asthma became much worse while she was working on the costume. She mentioned to Clarissa's parents that Clarissa had to take breaks, leaving the sculpture studio about every twenty minutes because of the dust and fumes.

Although there is some debate about the cause of her death, there is little argument about the events that led up to it. On Halloween night, Clarissa emerged from her bedroom as a giant cockroach and made her way slowly downstairs. Her mother, sitting in a recliner in the living room, glanced up from her newspaper. When she saw the fiberglass monstrosity rocking back and forth, and hanging on to the banister, she screamed. Clarissa's father came running from his study, a ballpoint pen still in his hand. He looked towards the stairs, grabbed his wife's arm, and both of them fled from the house. They ran blindly down the street filled with children in Halloween costumes, and finally took refuge with a neighbour. From there, worried sick about their daughter who was trapped in the house with a horrendous creature, unlike any they'd seen before, they called the police.

Within ten minutes, several police cars with sirens wailing, pulled up in front of the O'Land's house. They entered the premises to find a dented fiberglass case lying at the bottom of the stairs. There was no sign of Clarissa. A lot of commotion ensued. As the police grappled with the case, trying to cut it open, a group of paramedics arrived. They gathered at the bottom of the stairs and waited, their bags of emergency equipment within easy reach.

As the fiberglass gave way, everyone peered inside. The chocolate violinist, who worked as a paramedic several evenings a week, when she wasn't playing with the symphony orchestra, looked down at the strange sight. She saw a girl, whom she swore had the most beautiful face she'd ever laid eyes on in her life. A small flashlight shed light on the girl's right ankle. A book lay propped open on her chest. The chocolate violinist bent down to check whether Clarissa was breathing.

"Dear Reader, please don't die," she pleaded, sensing it was already too late.

# A Heart in Port

*Futile — the Winds —*
*To a Heart in port*
*Done with the Compass —*
*Done with the Chart!*

— Emily Dickinson

BEFORE LEDA LEFT Asia, Karel, who gave concerts all over the world said, "I'll wait for you." Tears dribbled down his cheek, on to the silver hair of his chest. "My Godness," he said again and again. Leda had to restrain herself from correcting his English. Correcting people's English was her job, but she took pleasure in Karel's mistakes, in hearing them again and again. As an Eastern European, he made different kinds of mistakes from her Asian students. He put a different slant of light on the English language. "My heart is with you whole the time. I am very much waiting for your phone call during the day." Leda wanted to believe him. But she guessed she'd be in Canada for longer than Karel could wait.

From what Leda remembered, her brother used to enjoy waking up. First thing in the morning, he surveyed his surroundings with wonder, marveled at the old Victorian house he had just bought, with floors of hemlock and three large bedrooms with barrel ceilings. Then, very slowly, things changed. Murray hated waking up. More days passed and things stayed much the same. Until one morning, Murray discovered the soft curve between his neck and shoulders had disappeared. He stayed quiet and watched the morning news until Leda came downstairs in her nightgown and slippers. He was sitting in the TV room. Leda could see only the back of his head, chunks of brown hair sticking up at odd angles.

"Want some breakfast?" she said. "Some scrambled eggs, maybe?"

"No," he said. "Come in here and look at me."

Leda padded into the TV room, rubbing her eyes. She glanced at an anchorman reporting an earthquake in LA, then at her brother wrapped in a blanket. His neck, from the edge of his jaw, was puffed up like a pillow.

"Oh, dear," said Leda.

"Feel," said Murray, touching his neck. Leda leaned over and poked. "Does it hurt?" she asked.

Murray shook his head. "What do you think it is?" he whispered. At that moment, he looked like a small child. Like the time their father yelled at him because he gave away all his birthday presents — a bicycle, a box of pencil crayons and a sketchpad, to a kid who lived down the street.

"I have no idea," said Leda, "but I think we should make a disappointment with Vikram. That's if we can get through Barbed Wire."

Leda and Murray spoke their own language. For years now his doctor's appointments had been disappointments, and his doctor had a passive aggressive receptionist called Barb.

"His neck is swollen and he needs to see Vikram as soon as possible," Leda explained on the phone. "It could be an infection and he might need some Zithromax."

"You think he has that Anthrax?" Barbed Wire said. The local news had an item about a ship detained in Halifax harbour because a sailor had died of Anthrax.

"No we don't think he has Anthrax. Look, can you put me through to Vikram? If you don't, I'll call his cell phone."

In the past, she had requested that Barbed Wire *kindly* ask Vikram to call them back, but somehow the messages never got passed on. Days later, Vikram would call back full of apologies. "There was some terrible, terrible mix up," he always said. Finally, he gave them the number to his direct line in case of emergencies.

After arranging a disappointment, Leda called Beth who had a car, thinking maybe she could give them a ride down to the medical clinic. Beth vacillated. She lived fifteen minutes away but had to cross the Halifax-Dartmouth bridge to reach their house, and pay a bridge toll of a dollar each way. "You guys realize," said Beth, "every time you need a ride somewhere it costs me two dollars." Bridge tolls were another controversial issue that figured prominently on the local news.

"Beth, this is serious," Leda replied. What she really wanted to say, really, really wanted to say, was that every time Beth came over and drank three or more beers and ate their food, it added up dollar-wise to more than the bridge toll. Instead, she said, "Please, Beth, it's a matter of life and death."

An hour later, at ten o'clock, Beth pounded up the front steps wearing jeans and an old work shirt covered with paint. Leda opened the front door and followed Beth into the TV room. When Beth laid eyes on Murray, her jaw dropped. Murray, in general, was a handsome man. He had a delicate nose and huge brown eyes, both of which made him appear slightly owlish. With his swollen neck, he looked more like a bullfrog. Strands of Beth's dirty blonde hair fell into her face as she leaned over to examine Murray more closely.

"Geez," she said. Then she went to the kitchen. Leda could hear the snap of Beth removing a tag from a can. There were two cans of ginger ale in the fridge, beside a jar of Miracle Whip. When Murray had an upset stomach, he craved ginger ale. Beth returned with a beer in her hand. "Aaahhhh," said Murray, "the breakfast of champions. Not a bad idea. Could you grab me one too?"

Leda sighed. This meant she would have to wait while Beth and Murray finished their drinks. Most of her time was swallowed up by the Waiting Monster and the Errand Monster, which seemed like brother and sister. Waiting at the Laundromat, waiting at the drugstore while pharmacists put together bags of Murray's medication, waiting in the waiting area while Murray had one of his disappointments. She rarely practiced the cello anymore.

Leda decided she wasn't going to hang around while Murray and Beth drank beer. She put on her sneakers and said she'd be back in twenty minutes. No matter what, she tried to go for a run every day. Like a dedicated gardener, she checked out her neighbourhood for signs of change. Everyday, something was a little bit different She put on her headphones. Sometimes she jogged along to classical music on the CDs Karel had given her. Other times she listened to tunes she'd grown up with. Leda walked down the front steps and turned right. At the end of the street, she jogged on the spot waiting for the lights to change. *I'm still standing* sang Elton John into her ears.

She ran a block, turned left, ran two more blocks. She passed Schooner's Fish and Chips. The place had three customers sitting at a table. Usually, it was empty and Mr. Schooner was standing outside in a spotty apron, smoking. Maybe they got a lot of delivery orders. She ran on. She noticed a shopping cart parked beside a pink house. It was lined with plastic bags from the grocery store. She jogged up to the cart and peered inside. Basil and rosemary. Who would think of filling a shopping cart with soil and planting herbs? She was used to seeing people who looked as though they were on social assistance dragging shopping carts full of empty containers to the recycling depot. She once saw a shopping cart in an art gallery, part of a large sculpture. But this herbal shopping cart really took the cake. She started running again, but a note taped to a shop window caught her eye. She stopped to read it.

*Dear Customers,*
*I know I haven't been around much lately. There are a lot of things going on in my life at the moment. You wouldn't believe it! When things calm down, I'll try to keep more regular hours. Thanks a ton for dropping by.*
*Yours truly, the Owner*

Boy, talk about the way *not* to run a business. The stores in Asia hardly ever closed. The shopkeepers were so dedicated. Suddenly, she missed those shops filled with persimmons, bean curd, and parasols. She ran four more blocks, the sun careening down on her forehead.

When she returned, Beth and Murray were ready to go. All three of them climbed into Beth's car. The back seat was filled with paint cans and brushes. "Those brushes are mine," Murray said, eyeing them. "You borrowed them a year ago, you should return them."

"Don't twist your head around. It might affect your neck," said Leda.

"Why?" Beth asked. "It's not as though you use them."

"That's not the point," Murray said. "They're mine. Some of those brushes are worth sixty dollars each. Every time you come over, you walk off with something and I never see it again. What about my mustard coloured corduroy shirt, the one Leda gave me for my birthday? What about my skill-saw?"

"I'll return your stuff," Beth said. "Don't worry."

"That's what you always say," said Murray, "and you never do."

When they entered the clinic, they checked in with Barb who averted her eyes and said nothing. "How can she ignore a man with no neck?" Beth whispered to Leda.

All three of them sat down in the waiting room. Beth picked up a battered copy of *People* magazine and began flipping through it. A kid wearing a yellow hockey shirt sat across from them. He had a bad cough and nasal drip. Every so often, a woman Leda assumed was his mother, passed him a tissue. Leda pointed out a sign taped to the front of the receptionist's desk. It showed a sketch of a teddy bear and read *Please Bear with Us.*

"What a lame sign," she said. "They should hire a good cartoonist from the *New Yorker* to make signs for doctor's offices. Laughter is supposed to be good for the health."

When Murray was still working on film sets, he'd spent a lot of time doing what he called "signage," for hotels, law courts, restaurants, whatever the sets happened to be. Last time they'd come to the clinic, he'd complained about the lack of signage. Upon arriving, he'd neglected to check in with Barb. He didn't think it was necessary. Barb saw the three of them walk in and sit down in the waiting area, and she knew Murray and Leda by name, not to mention sight. She'd left them waiting, long after the other patients in the waiting room had left the building.

Finally, Vikram had come out to look at the register. "I didn't realize you were here!" he said astonished.

"Barb didn't tell you?" Leda asked.

"They failed to report to me," said Barb to Vikram, by way of an explanation.

"*Report to you?*" Beth cried. "You're not our superior!"

"I think there's a problem with the signage," Murray piped up. "Nowhere do I see a sign that says upon arriving, please check in with the receptionist."

"There's been a terrible, terrible mix-up," Vikram said.

That visit had been a nightmare. Vikram informed them there was a black shadow on one of Murray's lung X-rays. It pointed to cancer, he explained, but not to hit the panic button. X-rays often lied. He arranged for Murray to have another set done as soon as possible.

"Cancer. Talk about a disappointment," Murray said as they left the clinic, and trooped across the parking lot. "Would you mind dropping by the liquor store?" he asked Beth.

Beth shook her head. Typically, she would have refused, the reason being she had to get back to work, to the film she was working on. Time's money, money's time, she would have said self-righteously. Murray would have pointed out she had a career thanks to him. That argument hadn't taken place, however. Even Beth, who prided herself on her resolutely unsentimental way of dealing with people and situations, showed evidence she was profoundly affected.

Her face hung and she didn't say much. When she stopped her car in front of the booth at the edge of the parking lot, Murray pulled out his wallet to pay. "Don't worry," she said, elevating her hips and digging into her pants' pocket, "I'll get it."

"That guy in the parking lot booth negotiated the mortgage on my house," said Murray. "He used to work at the bank on Carleton Road. Now he works in a parking lot. Can you believe it?

"He must have lost his job." Leda realized she had just stated the obvious.

"I bet he was fired," said Murray. "Otherwise they would have transferred him to one of the other branches. Welcome to the real world, buddy."

Leda had gazed out the car window. The black shadow on the X-ray would hang over their heads like a black cloud until they found out one way or another. She prayed Karel would call from Spain or France, wherever he happened to be. He didn't have that American way of trying to put a positive spin on things.

He never said things like, "It will all work out," or "You've got to be strong." He might say, "Oh my Godness," or "Maybe you should take a drink."

He would never say, "You'll get through this." Although he might say, "You will pass through it."

The second set of X-rays had turned out OK. That called for another trip to the liquor store.

Leda hoped this disappointment wouldn't be as disappointing as the last. But a neck swollen up like a balloon wasn't a good sign. She had skipped breakfast and her stomach was making screeching noises.

"They should have a sign saying. *Please Bear with Barbed Wire* and a picture of Auschwitz," Murray said loud enough for Barb to hear.

"Mom, what's an Ouchwich?" asked the kid in the hockey shirt.

"It's not important," said the kid's mother, handing over another Kleenex.

Jesus Christ, thought Leda. That kid must be about fifteen. What do they teach kids in school these days? How can a teenager never have heard of Auschwitz? Has he ever heard of Winston Churchill? He's heard of Wayne Gretsky, no doubt.

When Wayne Gretsky retired from hockey, Beth cried. That was the only time Leda had ever seen Beth cry. They were watching the news. The anchorman announced Gretsky's retirement. Beth burst into tears. Murray shouted at her. He said there were a lot of reasons to cry in the world, but Wayne Gretsky's retiring from hockey was not one of them.

Vikram entered the waiting room from a hallway. He looked particularly dapper. His hair was slicked back. He was wearing a grey suit with a blue and yellow polka dot tie. "Murray," he said. By now, Vikram was used to Murray and Company, knowing that Murray arrived accompanied by Beth or Leda or both.

Halfway down the hallway, he knocked on a door that belonged to his colleague. When the door opened, Vikram muttered something and a man in a white coat came out.

While Murray, Beth and Leda crowded into his office, Vikram consulted with his colleague in low tones. At one point, Vikram prodded Murray's neck area.

"I'm calling the emergency department at the hospital," Vikram said finally. "You need to go to emergency. This doesn't look good. May I give you a ride?"

Geez, Leda thought. When a doctor offers to give a patient a ride to the emergency department, things must be serious.

"That's OK," said Murray. "We have a car."

When they stopped to pay for the parking, Murray yelled out the car window to the man sitting in the booth. "Hey, you negotiated my mortgage, do you remember?" The man lowered his head to get a better look at Murray. "I think so," he said.

"Now, you're an Automotive Space-Allocation Specialist," Murray shouted. "That's what you should tell the guys at the bank, if you ever run into them. Tell 'em you're an A.S.S."

"I know you're upset, Murray, but that's no reason to go around insulting people," Leda said

"You think he understood anything I said? He never was the sharpest tack in the drawer."

"Sharpest knife in the drawer, sharpest tack in the box," said Leda.

"The deepest bowl in the cupboard," Beth added.

"You know where that comes from, the saying 'the sharpest tack in the box?" Murray asked. "It comes from when someone reaches blindly into a box of tacks and gets pricked."

"Gets pricked," Beth laughed.

"The word 'pricked' makes you laugh?" said Murray. "Boy, it doesn't take much, does it?"

That's what happened with Karel. Leda reached out blindly and ended up getting pricked. But not in that way. Falling in love with someone she had to leave to come back to Canada had pricked her deeply. It was a painful decision, more like a painful incision. There was no way Murray would agree to go into a nursing home. Even if he did, he'd drive all the nurses nuts and end up getting kicked out. Their father couldn't help. He had Parkinson's disease and their mother had died of cancer four years ago.

"I wonder if I'll have to go under the knife," Murray said softly. He entertained the prospect of having to spend some time in the hospital. He'd need an overnight bag with his bathrobe, slippers and some underwear.

Leda assured him he'd have everything he needed and desired. Murray said he expected a twenty-four hour vigil. He turned to look at Beth.

"I might have to work," Beth said.

At the emergency, Murray was rushed down a hallway on a stretcher. Beth and Leda followed. He was wheeled into a makeshift room with free walls. The emergency doctor entered right away. He said it looked as though Murray had a collapsed lung. He started asking questions, prepping for surgery. Leda's heart sank. It skipped like a pebble and then sank. The doctor wondered whether Murray could afford a private room after the surgery, if a surgical procedure was indeed necessary.

Then Murray was sent off for X-rays.

After he returned, the doctor entered the room brusquely. He asked if Murray would mind a few interns having a look at him.

"Bring 'em on," Murray said.

The doctor disappeared. Beth went to buy herself a coke from the machine in the hallway. Finally, the doctor returned with three interns. "OK," said the doctor, "take a look at this man. I want you to tell me what you think the problem is."

The three interns stared at Murray laid out on the stretcher. Standing there in identical white coats, they looked like a row of seagulls. They approached him and looked at his neck. Keeners, Leda thought.

"Have you switched colognes lately?" one of the interns asked. Leda looked at Beth. Like, *how did we go from a collapsed lung to switching colognes.*

"Yeah," said Murray, who had never worn cologne in his life. "Last week, I switched from Eternity to Miracle"

Karel wore cologne. He carried a bottle around in the pocket of his woolen jacket. If he had a beer at lunch and had to teach a class afterwards, he spritzed himself. He set a trend, actually. Suddenly all his Asian students started wearing cologne. In Canada, whenever Leda entered an office, she saw signs — *No Scent Makes Good Sense.* But, suddenly, owning a bottle of cologne, spraying oneself casually, struck her as incredibly European. After two months of inhaling Karel's cologne from

Spain, she bought herself a bottle of Eternity, and later a bottle of Miracle. After she returned to Halifax, Murray had spied the expensive bottles in the bathroom. "What the fuck are these?" he asked. "What? You're wearing perfume now?"

"Yeah," said another intern, focused and intense. "It looks like an allergic reaction to me."

The doctor looked at his feet. "Any other ideas?" The interns stared at him blankly, not responding. "I'll give you a bit more time. I'm going to get the X-ray results."

At that point, the room was pretty crowded — Beth, Leda, the three interns and Murray on the stretcher. "I don't have any other ideas," one of the interns confessed.

"If you give me sixty bucks, I'll tell you what the doctor thinks it is," said Murray. The interns exchanged glances. One raised his eyebrows. "I'm sorry," he said coolly, "we're not allowed to take bribes."

"Maybe you could just tell us?" said the intern with the cologne theory. He seemed a bit desperate.

"*Whooooooa no,*" said Murray. "If you're not willing to cough up the money, then you'll have to hazard another guess. And you know what a hazard guessing can be when it comes to fatal lung disease."

"Fatal lung disease!" the cologne theorist exclaimed. His eyes lit up like a game show contestant.

"He has fatal lung disease," echoed another one of the interns. "Is it really fatal?"

"You'll have to guess," Murray replied. "I can't give you all the answers."

The doctor returned with a smile on his face. He assured Murray it wasn't what they thought, not as bad as they expected.

The least vocal of the interns mumbled something about lung disease. They thought the swelling might be connected to lung disease.

The doctor seemed somewhat relieved. He explained to the interns that initially, he had suspected a collapsed lung. However, that wasn't the case.

A week later, Beth was exuberant, flushed with excitement. She stood in the middle of the TV room, her hands on hips. "I worked my ass off, today," she announced.

"I can still see your ass," said Murray. Beth wasn't fat but she was stocky and pear shaped.

Once, Beth was Murray's girlfriend. They tried living together, but things hadn't worked out. Murray was demanding and temperamental, prone to throwing lawn chairs off decks and across the backyard. That he was ill made him even worse. When Leda made freshly roasted coffee in the morning, he complained the smell made him nauseous. "It's not a smell, it's an aroma," Leda said.

Couldn't she make instant coffee, Falcon's crystals, Murray wanted to know. No, she couldn't. A freshly ground French roast and Falcon's crystals weren't the same thing, although Murray insisted they were. She had come all the way back from Asia to take care of him. Put her teaching career on hold. She wasn't about to give up her freshly roasted coffee.

He said if she continued to make coffee in the morning, he would have to take something for nausea — this on top of all the other medication he was taking. Next time, she went to the drugstore, could she pick him up an anti-nauseant and ask the pharmacist if it was OK to take them with steroids?

The anti-nauseants were packaged in a pink box that said *For The Prevention and Treatment of Nausea, Vomiting or Dizziness Due to Motion Sickness.*

Motion sickness. Murray hadn't left the house in over six months, except to go to the doctor. He barely moved from his chair in the TV room. When Leda brought the pills home, Murray examined the black print on the back of the box. "Warning," he read out loud in an authoritative voice, "do not take this product if you have glaucoma or chronic lung disease." Leda took the box from Murray and read the warning herself. It also said to avoid alcoholic beverages. And he was incapable of doing that.

"Murray, it's up to you whether you take the pills or not. I'm not switching to instant coffee," Leda said. Often, she needed pills or a shot of vodka just to deal with him. Murray was an enterprising, pragmatic person. He was used to pushing against the world, heading large crews of painters on film sets. Now he could no longer work, he pushed against her.

Or, he pushed against Beth, who occupied a fuzzy area between a friend and an ex-girlfriend.

At least three times a week, Beth dropped by the house, sometimes to watch movies, quarrel, or dredge up the past. Beth was a rigid scorekeeper, a cataloguer of wounds. When Beth worked for Murray, she became enraged by what she perceived as unfair treatment and took to storming around the film set. "Just let her cool off," Murray advised the other painters. "Give Macbeth half an hour and she'll calm down."

Beth working for Murray was ancient history now. Owing to the materials he'd worked around over the years — paint fumes, shellacs and thinners — his lungs were covered with cysts, which were metamorphosing into scar tissue. The doctors said he had about five years to live. In a short period of time, he had lost his health, his job, and now, because of money problems, he could lose his house.

He was hooked up to an oxygen tank. Murray called it his lung. *Leda, could you clean the filter on my lung?* Leda cleaned the filters on his lung, she bought groceries, she did the cooking.

When Beth knocked on the door, Leda was cutting up carrots for a soup. "Feel my pants," said Beth, strutting into the kitchen, "they feel like lizard skin." When Murray worked in the film industry, his denims ended up the same way. Once, he took the pair of jeans he'd worn for weeks and cut them up. He collaged them onto a stretched canvas, a painting he was working on. The pieces of denim encrusted with paint merged with the cloth of the canvas, over which Murray layered colour after colour, so the surface became one strange scaly skin.

Beth stood in the living room within earshot of the kitchen and the TV room. "There's this painter called Rory," Beth began. "At eight o'clock this morning he went around labelling cans of paint so we'd know what colours were inside. He labelled the lids. *Anyone* who has worked in this industry for any amount of time knows better than to label paint lids."

Beth flung her arms around, dramatizing her indignation. "By noon, the lids got all mixed up and ended up on the wrong cans of paint. Guess who had to spend an hour opening and closing paint cans to find the right colour?"

"Not Macbeth?" Murray droned from the living room.

Beth ignored his comment and continued, describing how Antonio had assigned her the task of re-labeling the cans but

then gave the job to Kevin as he wanted her to do some touch-
ups that required skill."

Leda threw the carrots in the soup and washed some celery.
A month ago, Beth had been terrified of working for Antonio.
Murray and Antonio were enemies. When Murray was working,
they competed for the same jobs. Murray was local talent, from
Nova Scotia, whereas Antonio had come from New York. One
night at the bar, Antonio called Murray a small town boy who
knew nothing. Murray called Antonio a stupid old Wop who
couldn't handle the Big Apple.

Beth needed work, but she had worried about asking Antonio
for a job. Antonio might have heard she was Murray's friend
or ex-girlfriend. He might belittle her or give her the most
unsavory tasks. "You'll be fine," Murray had assured her. "Just
don't call him a Wop. As a matter of fact, don't use any words
that rhyme with Wop. Drop, Mop, Slop."

As it turned out, Beth had nothing to worry about. Antonio
actually *liked* her. Beth was elated, as this meant she would
continue to make a couple of hundred dollars a day. "I think
Antonio gets a kick out of me," Beth said happily. "Today, I
knocked over a bucket of paint and he just laughed."

"Ha, ha, ha," said Murray. "Knocking over a can of paint.
That's really funny."

Leda wished Beth could curb her enthusiasm. She insisted
on carrying on like a pot boiling over, oblivious to the effect it
had on Murray. Beth *knew* how much Murray missed working.
When Murray met Beth, she was in art school, slinging beer
in a bar. Who gave Beth her first job, her second job, her third
job, until she had enough hours to become a union member?
He basically handed her a career on a silver platter. Yet, Beth

insisted on strutting through the door in her paint clothes, regaling them with anecdotes they didn't want to hear, inviting herself for dinner. As if they could afford it.

Feel sorry for her, Leda told herself. Feel sorry for anyone that brash and insensitive. To most people, Beth came across like a bulldozer, determined to level anything that stood in her way. Nowadays, people called it survival instinct. But, there was a good chance Beth could end up like Murray. Beth was only twenty-eight, but whenever she stayed the night, and slept in the bedroom upstairs, Leda could hear her hacking and coughing. She worked around the same materials Murray had. Even though she wore a mask, the cartridges didn't filter out everything. Beth also had asthma and was constantly honking away on inhalers.

She had been diagnosed with asthma and allergies when she was seven years old. The doctors advised her mother and her mother's boyfriend to quit smoking, get rid of their cat and pull up all the shag carpets. Her mother and her mother's boyfriend kept on smoking. Moreover, her mother didn't tear up the carpets, as she liked the way the shag felt under her feet. But they had no problem getting rid of the cat. "They put it down," said Beth one night on the porch, while she and Leda were drinking gin and tonics. "I loved that cat so much. I couldn't understand it. I cried three days straight."

Whenever Leda started to suspect that the only person Beth cared about was herself, she thought about how much Beth had loved that cat.

Charm, that's what Beth lacked, charm and subtlety.

Karel oozed charm and manners. In Asia, there were always receptions, small parties, after one of the musicians gave a concert. Weeks before one of Karel's big concerts, the musicians were wondering where to hold the reception. Marek, the Polish violinist offered to have it at his flat, but he was close to sixty. Preparing for a reception would have been a lot of work for him, on top of his teaching. Leda offered to host the gathering in her flat. During the evening, Karel kissed the back of her hand and bowed slightly. *"I am much obliged,"* he said. *"Thank you so much."*

After the guests had left, Karel stayed and helped her clean up. There were wine glasses and scrunched up serviettes everywhere. Bouquets of flowers lay heaped up in every corner. Five hours ago, Karel had played the Elgar *Cello Concerto* and now he helped her scrape chocolate icing from dessert plates and into the garbage.

Later that night, Karel made love to her. No one had ever made love to her like that before. Which may have said something about Karel or something about every other lover she'd ever had.

In the evenings, they drank chilled vodka, discussing everything from taxes in the Czech Republic to cello repertoire. Leda mined him for his opinions. What did he think about the tenor from Hungary? *Well, you know the saying, every instrument needs a space to make a sound, with him it's in his head.*

Karel, in turn, wanted to know everything about her past. What the house she grew up in looked like. The years she spent in Denmark. Describe Murray. Was their mother short or tall? This Beth, was she a nice person? Why Leda decided to travel to Asia and teach. Why she stopped playing the cello. What she usually had for breakfast when she lived in Canada. He absorbed detail after detail.

Eventually, Karel offered to give her cello lessons.

Leda was appalled. She hadn't touched the cello for ages. "It's too late," she said.

"Too late for what?" Karel asked, throwing up his hands. "Play for your own enjoyment. To be a professional musician is a very hard life."

Karel taught advanced students who practiced eight hours a day. Many of his Asian students practiced twelve hours a day. Karel understood that kind of work ethic, built into Japanese and Korean cultures, where grocers worked long hours so their kids could have a stab at a better life. It reminded him of his own Czech family with its roots in Eastern European poverty. The whole concept drove Leda crazy. Why waste his time giving her lessons when he could be giving an extra hour to a student who really needed it?

"Look," said Karel, "Here, at the Academy, I have ten students. One girl is very talented and another girl she is not much talented or serious by comparison. I tell the administrator the very talented girl should have more lessons. Two-hour lessons twice a week. He says no, no, no, I must give the not much talented girl more lessons because she needs them more. That is time being wasted!" Karel went on to argue he spent his free time with Leda, so why not throw in a few lessons? "It is obvious," he said.

Yes, Karel had charm. He was not the kind of person who would bounce through the door and assume he was staying for dinner. First of all, he wouldn't bounce, and second, he wouldn't assume. For him, it was obvious.

To preempt Beth's digging into the pork chops, Leda decided to invite her for dinner before she could invite herself. "Beth, would you like to stay for dinner?" Leda asked. "I'm making a soup and I think we have enough pork chops." It made Leda feel better, gave her more control over the situation.

Murray picked up on Leda's strategy immediately. He started singing, "You Took The Words Right Out Of My Mouth" from Meatloaf's *Bat Out Of Hell*. "You took the food right out of our mouths!"

After dinner, Beth put on her coat announced she was going to The Middle Deck to meet some of the painting crew for drinks.

Murray said he wanted to come along. Now the bars in Halifax had designated no-smoking areas, it wouldn't be a problem.

"Don't be so stupid," said Beth. "You can't take an oxygen tank into a tavern."

"We'll take my portable oxygen," Murray said defiantly. "Besides I'm sure I can go for two or three hours without it. My breathing's been pretty good this week. Please take me. I know all the painters. They'd be happy to see me."

"You're not coming," said Beth.

"Is Antonio going to be there?" Murray asked. "Is that what you're worried about?"

"No, Antonio is not going to be there," replied Beth. "The fact is, you haven't gone anywhere in six months besides the hospital, and now you want to go to a bar? That's crazy."

"She's got a point," said Leda. "I'm not sure a bar is a good idea for your first outing."

At the same time, she knew why Murray thought it was the perfect idea. He used to love going to the bar after a long week of twelve-hour days. He sat at the head of the table, surrounded by his painters, loyal knights in paint-encrusted armour. But, it wasn't just that. Murray hadn't had any social interaction in a long time. No doubt, he was nervous and figured a few drinks would help ease the tension. Nevertheless, a bar wasn't the best idea. Then again, she thought, if Murray had trouble breathing, Beth could always drive him home.

"Beth, that's not the real reason," Murray protested. "There's another reason you don't want me to come along. You're afraid certain female painters will flirt with me, like they always did. You like the fact I'm trapped in this house night and day."

"That's not the reason," Beth groaned. She checked her reflection in the mirror above the fireplace and started applying mascara.

"You're lying," Murray said to Beth. "You always lie." He went on. When he called her in the evening, on her mobile phone, he could tell she was in the bar. He could hear the sound of the jukebox playing old hits and the clinking of glasses. Yet, according to Beth, she was at home. He said she came from a family of liars, so it was no big surprise she was a liar herself.

"*What are you talking about?*" Beth demanded, turning around, the mascara wand pointing in the direction of the ceiling.

Leda guessed the real reason. Murray was unpredictable. Beth was worried Murray might say or do something that would jeopardize her job. After all, if Beth brought him to the bar, he was officially her guest. Whatever he did would reflect on her. Murray might drink too much and pontificate about

Antonio's lack of professionalism and this would get back to Antonio. Beth didn't trust the people she worked with. She had told Leda that.

"When our mother died," said Murray, "or do you forget?"

"No, I don't forget," Beth said angrily, "I went to the funeral."

"When our mother died," Murray continued, "your mother called me and said she wanted to send some flowers. I told her we weren't accepting flowers, that in lieu of flowers, to make a donation to the breast cancer foundation. She said she'd be sure to do it. Your mother didn't donate. Months later, I got a list from the breast cancer foundation and her name wasn't on it. I couldn't believe it! The next day, I called her and thanked her for making a donation. And you know what she said? She said, 'It was the least I could do.' *The least I can do.* What a fucking liar!"

Leda started getting upset. "*Murray,* Beth can't help what her mother does or doesn't do. She can't control whether her mother makes a donation."

"Murray," Beth said with calculated calm, "I've worked my ass off this week, and I want to spend a few hours relaxing and drinking with the crew. If you have breathing problems, then you'll insist I drive you home and there goes my night out, right out the window."

"I'll take a cab," said Murray miserably.

"You're not coming," she replied. "You'll make a scene if nothing else. Once you've had a few drinks, you always make a scene." Beth turned to the mirror and started applying lipstick. Then her mobile phone rang. She answered it, providing information about times and the meeting place. "That was

Kevin," she said after disconnecting. "He's meeting me here. He wants a ride down to The Middle Deck."

"That means I'm coming," said Murray joyously. He went into the bathroom next to the kitchen, leaving the door open a crack. Leda could hear him brushing his teeth.

"Leda, could you go upstairs and get my blue jeans with the rip in the leg and my paisley shirt?" he asked.

"Sure," said Leda.

"YOU'RE NOT COMING!" Beth screamed from the TV room.

Murray changed out of his sweat pants and t-shirt. After that, he packed his portable oxygen tank into a sporty blue knapsack designed to hold the capsule. Then he sat down in his chair and waited.

Finally, a knock at the door. Murray jumped up to answer it. Leda followed him into the foyer. A girl in a blue tunic smiled brightly. She had brown eyes shaped like almonds and red wavy hair. She held a box full of chocolate bars. "So cute," Leda gushed. She thought of Karel, what a daughter of his might look like.

"Wanna buy a bar?" the girl asked.

"No, I wanna go to the bar," said Murray and shut the door.

"That wasn't very nice," said Leda. "You could have at least said, 'No, thank you.'"

Ten minutes later, another knock. Beth answered it. "Kev," she said, "let's go." Murray got out of his chair. "Kevin! Good to see ya!" Kevin was a sweet kid with blue startled eyes. He was about twenty-six or so. "Murray," said Kevin, shaking Murray's hand, "how ya doin, man? I haven't seen ya in awhile. How's yer health?"

"Never been better," said Murray confidently. "Kevin, who gave you your first job in the film industry?"

"You did," said Kevin. "Murray, man, do you think that's the kind of thing I'd forget? You probably don't like the fact I'm working for Antonio, but I gotta make ends meet. Is that the problem, that I'm working for Antonio?"

"No," said Murray. "I don't give a shit. You gotta do what you gotta do. I just want to come out to the bar with you tonight? Will you take me?"

"Of course!" said Kevin.

Beth gave Kevin a look. "He wants to take his oxygen tank into the bar. He hasn't been out of the house in six months. He's *not* coming with us."

Kevin looked at the portable oxygen tank in the blue knapsack. "I *guess* we can take the oxygen tank. I've never seen anyone in a bar with an oxygen tank but there's no rules against it, not as far as I know."

"It's absurd," said Beth.

"I probably won't even need it," Murray said.

"You're not coming!" Beth exclaimed.

"You treat me like a child. You can't stop me from coming. I'm a free man."

"That's true," Kevin pointed out. "He's a free man."

"Well, I can certainly stop you from getting in my car," said Beth.

"Then, I'll take a cab," said Murray. "You'll make me spend seven dollars on a cab downtown when you're going there anyway."

"This'll cause all kinds of problems," Beth complained. "Tibby smokes and she's coming. Bobby Cochrane's coming and he smokes. They'll want to sit in the smoking section where we always sit."

"Not Bobby-the-Cock Cochrane," Murray groaned. "What an annoying prick he is."

Beth looked at Kevin and then Leda for support. "Yeah, and then you'll say something sarcastic to Bobby and the two of you will end up in a vicious argument. Then Bobby will wanna fight."

"I won't say a word," said Murray. "Not a word."

Beth rolled her eyes to the ceiling. "Oh yeah, that's just like you. What was it the bartender used to say? Whenever you were sitting in the bar and Bobby walked in, the bartender said to Bobby, 'Do I call the police now or later?'"

"What's Bobby gonna do? Hit a dying man?" asked Murray.

Beth threw up her hands. "OK," she said, addressing Kevin. "But, he's your responsibility. If anyone asks who brought him along, *you* did, not me."

"'No problem," said Kevin, patting Murray on the back. "I got no problem with that."

"Thanks, mate," Murray said, happily. "Leda, you wanna come as well?"

"Oh, I don't know," Leda replied with little enthusiasm. "I'm kinda tired." It was true. In the morning, she picked up pieces of tarpaper from the back lawn. The neighbours were having their roof fixed, and tarpaper kept flying over the fence like bat wings. Then she went to grocery store. Did laundry at the Laundromat. After that, Murray asked her to fill a tub with warm water because he wanted to soak his feet and scale off the dead skin. Her first instinct was to tell him to get off his ass and do it himself. But actually, she wasn't sure what he could do, should do for himself anymore. Not after what the emergency doctor said a week ago.

"It's subcutaneous emphysema," the doctor had announced to Murray and everyone in the makeshift room. "Something ruptured and air leaked out of your lungs and under your skin. It should dissipate within a few days."

"So no surgery!" Murray said happily.

"Now," he said, addressing Murray, "go home and take it easy, lots of rest. Absolutely, *no* air travel and *no* scuba diving!"

Both Beth and Leda laughed. Murray was the last guy you'd find in a scuba diving suit. Plus, he was terrified of flying.

"And no heavy lifting," the doctor had added.

Leda wasn't sure whether carrying a tub of water constituted heavy lifting. It didn't seem worth finding out, anyway. She placed a tub of lukewarm water in the TV room, in front of the Murray's chair. After soaking his feet, he announced he wanted a pedicure. Murray's feet belonged to another world, owing to his poor circulation and the steroids he had to take. When he removed his socks, skin flakes eddied around the room. No matter how hard she worked at removing the layers of dead skin from his soles, she couldn't seem to reach rock bottom. His toenails were infected with fungus and unnaturally thick, impossible to cut. Even going to the laundromat was preferable to messing around with his feet.

Painstakingly, he tried to peel off a sock. The cotton stuck like Velcro to the crust of his ankles. While he worked on the other sock, Leda went in search of a towel. After the initial soaking of his feet, she'd have to change the cloudy water. In the meantime, he'd need a towel to put his wet feet on. All the towels were clean. She had washed them, folded them, and stacked them in the laundry closet upstairs. It seemed a pity to sacrifice a clean towel to one of Murray's pedicures. Any old dirty towel would do.

She found a pink striped hand towel and brought it downstairs and into the TV room. "Look," said Murray, crinkling his nose, "my big toenail came off with my sock!" He held up the toenail for her inspection. It was thick and yellow.

"Gross!" she said, backing away. The rest of his toenails were more discoloured than she remembered. Another nail might fall off any minute. "I'm sorry, Murray, but you'll have to do your feet yourself. I can't take it!"

"Oh, please," he begged, "it's hard for me to bend over and it takes lots of energy." He stuck a foot in the air, close to her face.

Leda left Murray to deal with his feet and went upstairs to practise her cello.

When she started practising in Asia, the tips of her fingers on her left hand were as soft as pillows. Useless. It took months before they became calloused from the strings, like little hammers.

The first time she played for Karel, she chose Schumann's *Three Fantasy Pieces.* Closing her eyes to concentrate, she had the feeling she was sleepwalking through a house she had lived in years ago. She could divine the locations of the rooms, she knew if she walked a certain distance, there would be a staircase that curved to the right. At one point, Karel asked her to stop, and the spell was broken. He asked her to play *The Swan* by Saint-Saëns.

"*The Swan?*" she said with disbelief. She played *The Swan* when she was eight years old! It was a simple piece but difficult to play well — to achieve the right tone, slow and burnished. To make the lines sing of sadness and nostalgia. To give each note its due respect, to weight the climaxes. Few cellists left *The Swan* behind completely. Even when she fifteen, Leda returned to *The Swan* now and again, especially when her friends requested she play something. It was a crowd pleaser. Like most cellists, she knew it by heart.

So she played *The Swan*, as Karel had asked.

For the next six months, Karel insisted she play nothing but *The Swan*. She felt humiliated as if he were asking her to put the training wheels back on her bicycle. But, that wasn't the worst of it. He relegated her playing to the upper section of her bow. From the middle of the bow to the tip. To fit all the notes into half a bow that would ordinarily require a full bow, was sheer hell.

She questioned whether Karel had a sadomasochist streak. The rest of his students were playing concertos and here was she, grappling with *The Swan*.

"Leda, I think this swan sounds more like a goose," Karel said, monitoring her progress.

Leda agreed. She became increasingly frustrated. At times she insisted it was impossible — trying to play it with half a bow. He wouldn't expect someone to cook a dinner for seventeen guests, using only one pot.

"Not impossible," Karel said. "Play closer to the bridge. It's all in your bowing arm. Pretend your right hand is a paintbrush. That's how you make smooth bow transitions."

She reminded Karel he had said she should play for her own enjoyment. There was no enjoyment to be had. Karel told her to wait. Even enjoyment costs something, he assured her. "Not enjoyment like going to the cinema, but let's say other kind of enjoyment. This Russian cellist, Gregor Piatigorsky said, *cellists are unmistakable because there is a touch of nostalgia that can be recognized like a scar, from a long battle — often a losing one — against the odds of their instrument.*"

Later, when Leda played *The Swan* to Karel's satisfaction, he sat there beaming at her. "It looks like your goose has turned into a swan. A beautiful sad aristocratic swan. Congratulations! Next we will work on Bach's *Third Suite.*"

After *The Swan*, it seemed as though Leda had a large park to play in. She could use her entire bow, from tip to frog. One afternoon, she played the prelude of Bach's suite, while Karel paced back and forth in his flat. He moved a lot when he was teaching. "Less choppy," Karel cried out.

"OK," he said after she played the passage several times, "Now, why it is?"

"Why it is?" asked Leda, confused.

"Why it is you play it that way? You play with too much head," he said, tapping his temple. "There is truth of the head and truth of the heart. The last is always truer."

Leda laughed.

"It is not a joke," he said, frowning.

"No, I know," she said, trying to be serious.

When she woke up that morning, a Saturday, she found a note from Karel.

*My dearest,*
*It is sad, but I have to go to teach. You just sleep like a baby. Serve*
*yourself. I bought water so you can make coffee. If you wake up*
*call my studio. We should think about good lunch. And about good*
*sex. Do you want to go somewhere? And as well I can show you the*
*place you can buy paintings I know you want to send to Canada.*
*And as well we could have a lesson. Just think what we can do. It*
*has to be a lazy, nice day. But first of all have a rest!*
*I kiss you so much*
*Love*
*K*
*P.S. Isn't it something giving a head at 5 a.m.? (by the way)*

Leda laughed out loud. Giving a head. She went in search of the water he bought. She opened the front door and sat on the one front step, gazing at the trumpet flowers, waiting for the water to boil.

The same evening, she sat at Karel's kitchen table. Karel was drinking red wine, while she made a list. She drew a line down the middle of a piece of paper. On one side she listed the reasons she should move back to Halifax.

Murray
Dad
Good seafood
The medicare system

On the other side, she listed the reasons she should move to Europe with Karel. This side of the list was weighty with reasons.

Love
Having a baby?
Leading a normal life
Great concerts
Architecture to die for
Less rain
Beautiful coffee shops
Good, cheap wine

She read the list out loud to Karel. He looked sad. He said lists were fine for shopping but not for big decisions. He reminded her of his words earlier that day. The truth of the head and the truth of the heart, what the great cellist, Pablo Casals, always talked about with his students. But which she seemed to consider a kind of joke.

"No, no, it wasn't that," she sighed. "I was thinking about *head*, the truth of oral sex. My mind does that, it goes in its own direction at the most inopportune moments."

"Oh," he said.

Feeling a terrible wave of premature nostalgia, she scrawled 'Great sex' at the end of the list for reasons she should move to Europe. Then, she crossed it out, resenting its proximity to the word 'cheap' in the words 'Good cheap wine.' Besides, great sex fell under the love umbrella anyway.

Karel was right. The list was ridiculous. How could she weigh the prospect of a happy life with Karel, of having a baby — "I want to be the father of your children," he often whispered, as she fell asleep — against the guilt she might feel if something terrible happened to Murray?

Leda spent so much time at Karel's flat, she had given Murray the phone number there, in case he needed to talk. Murray had called an hour before. He conjured up scenes and concerns that seemed surreal, completely discordant with Leda's present existence. He complained the basement in his house had flooded. The roommate he had had for many years, who paid half his mortgage, had moved out after confessing living with Murray was too depressing. He couldn't deal with the mood swings that were the side effects of Murray's medication. Also, he was sick of running errands, even though he knew Murray needed them run. Plus, he was sick of hearing Beth and Murray argue. Summing everything up, the roommate said he needed his own space.

Nowhere else would Murray find a roommate like that. He had been amenable over the years, but Leda guessed he had reached his saturation point.

Then Murray mentioned he hadn't eaten in three days. There was no food in the house. He had had an argument with Beth, and now she refused to speak to him, let alone do shopping for him.

"What about the Meals-on-Wheels service you had going?"

"I told you, it was terrible!" said Murray. "They brought deep-fried fish that was ninety percent batter and carrots that tasted like cardboard, and charged me five bucks a meal. I've never eaten that way in my life."

"Well, it's better than starving," said Leda.

Now the roommate was gone there would be other issues, small crises that in Murray's world would amount to the sky falling. Who would run to the store when the batteries in his remote control paddle died? Who would go the liquor store? Who would buy his painkillers with codeine?

"I need you to come home, I need my Meals-on-Heels." Leda could tell he was drinking. "The only time I eat properly is when you come home for the summer."

"It sounds as though you're having a few libations," said Leda, trying not to sound critical. "How did you get whatever you're drinking?"

"I paid a cab driver to go the liquor store for me," Murray replied matter-of-factly.

When Leda hung up the phone, she told Karel Murray had nothing to eat and was hiring taxis to bring him booze. Murray must have some cash in the house, she surmised. When the cash ran out and if he couldn't get someone to drive him to a bank machine, he'd probably give his bank card and secret number to the cab driver. She knew her brother, and it was a distinct possibility.

"Oh, my Godness!" said Karel. "It is a world I cannot imagine."

Murray's arrival created quite a sensation. As soon as Kevin pushed open the glass door and Murray followed, a table of painters, sitting by the entrance stood up and started clapping. "Your first standing ovation," Leda commented. The owner of the bar gave Murray a hug and offered to buy him a drink. Murray painted the bar, years ago, before it opened, during a lapse between film jobs. The owner wanted something funky. Murray painted the walls a streaky bird egg blue, using various washes to give the paint a vertical orientation. It made the room seem bigger, created the illusion of space, he explained to the owner at the time. The walls looked rained on by paint and water, the colour thinning in certain areas.

Murray introduced Leda to the painters, some of whom she already knew. Rory, Laura who had a high pitched laugh, Tibby, who as far as Beth was concerned, spent too much time flirting with the carpenters. Don, and Annie.

After sitting down, Leda ordered a vodka from the bartender. Murray had a beer and a gin and tonic, which he sipped intermittently. He sat sandwiched between Kevin and Annie who had very short bangs Leda had heard referred to as fringes.

Murray seemed happy. He entertained Annie by recounting a "terrible, terrible" mistake he made when painting the bar, although he didn't know it until weeks later, just before the bar was supposed to open. The building inspector was wandering around while the bar's manager, a slightly manic man who apparently hadn't slept a wink since he quit drinking, was in the process of giving the bartenders a pep talk. Murray did great imitations. Leda often thought he missed his calling as an actor. He started mimicking the manager, his character voice commanding the attention of everyone at the table. *When clients come in here, they wanna feel like it's their first home, not their second home, but their first home. They wanna feel cared for, acknowledged and recognized and it's up to you guys to give them that down home feeling.*

Then the building inspector started to walk in a circle, his eyes focused on the ceiling. He called the manager over, disrupting the pep talk. The building inspector complained that someone had painted over the sprinkler system.

"Sprinkler system?" asked Tibby, lighting a cigarette. Leda realized they were sitting in the smoking section, but it wasn't very smoky and because it was hot, someone had propped the door open.

"Yeah, look over there," said Murray pointing to a mechanism installed in the ceiling. "In case of fire."

"You painted over the sprinkler system?" asked Don.

Murray shrugged. "I thought it was ugly, so I decided to paint over it. Unfortunately, the paint plugged up the holes in the fan. I didn't notice the holes at the time, they were so small. Anyway, the building inspector said a new sprinkler system had to be installed before the bar could open. Otherwise the place was a fire hazard. The manager had a fit because the bar was supposed to open that night. He tried to bribe the building inspector with drinks, but it didn't work."

Annie giggled. She toyed with the silk scarf knotted around her neck.

A good looking man with black curly hair staggered from the bar against which he'd been leaning, to the table. He stood there, swaying slightly. "Hey, Bobby," said Don.

"Bobby-the-cock-Cochrane," Murray muttered under his breath to Annie.

Beth walked in and sat down at the table between Leda and Kevin. She said it had taken her twenty minutes to find a parking space. And, man, could she ever use a drink.

"I give the best head in Halifax!" Bobby announced.

Leda hoped Murray would keep his mouth shut. Leda could imagine him saying something like, yeah, that's what Antonio says. Murray had the same sense of humour as their father. Or as their father used to. He still tried to tell jokes. But because his mind was going, he often forgot the punch lines. His eyes moved back and forth wildly and then the jokes dwindled away, as if they had run out of batteries. Murray claimed the jokes had become a form of abstraction. Murray loved abstraction. For his Master's in Fine Arts, Murray created nothing but white-on-white paintings, paintings that were so minimalist they just seemed to buzz.

True to his word, Murray didn't say a word. Bobby wandered back to the bar.

"He's so good looking," said Tibby. "He knows it too."

"His legs are kinda short, though," observed Annie. "When I lived on the prairies, most of the guys had these nice long cowboy legs. All the guys in the Maritimes have short legs in proportions to their torsos."

"It's because most of us are descended from fishermen," said Rory. "Short legs are better for keeping your balance on a boat, so they became a dominant genetic trait."

"Is that *true?* Beth gasped.

"Oh, my God," Murray groaned, rolling his eyes.

"Sure, it's true," said Rory. "Can you imagine 'em cowboys on their long legs working on a boat? They'd just tip over."

Leda wished she'd stayed at home. What if she missed one of Karel's phone calls? He was back at home now, in Prague, after a concert in Warsaw. When he asked the simple question, "How are you?" she didn't know how to answer anymore. Compared to what? Compared to people who were starving in the world? Compared to when they were together in Asia, the happiest version of herself she had ever known? She had lost her emotional orientation.

Karel seemed to understand that. When she sighed, he said, "I hope you are OK, more or less. I think about you whole the time."

Murray was sticking his fingers in his gin and tonic trying to snag a wedge of lemon. Annie had said she wanted to squeeze a bit of lemon juice in her glass of water. Lemon was her favourite flavour she informed Murray. Lemon gelato, lemon-flavoured mineral water, lemon candies. Murray managed to fish out the lemon but then dropped it on the floor.

"Shit," he said.

Annie laughed. She took Murray's hand, his thumb and index finger and started sucking on them. "Mmmmm," she said, "they're lemony. I just want to taste lemon."

"You could ask the bartender for some lemon," Beth snapped. She was livid. Laura and Tibby exchanged glances.

Leda felt a certain amount of satisfaction. Beth wanted to distance herself from Murray on this occasion, but it wasn't working in her favour. Reasonably, she couldn't blame Murray for allowing his hand to be grabbed. And, Annie had no idea Beth and Murray had ever been involved.

Murray looked at Beth with a playful vengeance. As if to say, see, you *were* afraid women would flirt with me. And also, women still find me attractive. Despite the fact I'm bloated from steroids.

Leda, whispering, cautioned Beth not to overreact. After all, it wasn't Murray's fault his finger was co-opted. And, booze can affect people in weird ways. Leda wasn't a peacemaker by nature, but she realized that, if she didn't do some damage control pretty quickly, her own peace and quiet could be in jeopardy. Without thinking, she could chart the course of the arguments over the next week. Beth would say Murray had made a fool of her in front of Laura, Tibby, Rory, and Kevin. Murray would accuse Beth of never returning his stuff.

To ease the tension, Don changed the subject. He started talking about the film set they were working on.

Leda's mind wandered in the direction of Karel. She felt a flutter of white wings. That morning, a postcard had arrived. It had been sent from Warsaw and depicted a black and white photo of a pile of rubble, what was once the Royal Castle. In bold print: 1945. Below this, another photograph, but in colour, showing the castle reconstructed, its five-winged body with clock tower. Leda turned the postcard over.

*My Love,*

*I just gave my concert in Warsaw. It was a good concert, but I feel like Mr. Nobody. This picture on the postcard in 1945 is like my life now. I told my wife I will leave her but she says she will never give me a divorce. I want to have children with Leda and love her more than I expected. In Prague, I cried so many times thinking about you. The only good news is my daughter has very high marks and is accepted into the best university. Honey — come to Europe — we have to see each other. Karel*
*P.S. I am very much waiting for you while you are in Canada.*

Leda wanted to believe him, but the fact is, men don't wait. Women are different. They have a long history of waiting — waiting for lovers and husbands to come back from war, dangerous missions.

In movies, romantic novels, it's the women who wait. Wait and weave, wait and spin, in rooms filled with shadows and mirrors. It's what they've been taught. They've built up their endurance. Yes, women can wait, as if it were inbred.

Men don't wait, at least not in the same way. They think about waiting, have a strong drink and move on. Men know better than to procrastinate happiness. Life is short and accidents happen. Waiting is a woman's game. Boys learn this early, and it sticks with them.

# THE GRAVEYARD

THERE ARE THREE entrances, like two eyes and a mouth. A roadway runs from one eye to the other, straight through the middle of the cemetery. There is another roadway as well, that runs from the "mouth" entrance in a chain link fence to meet the first roadway where, let's say, a nose might be. And finally there is a third roadway, and almost perfect square containing the grassed area of trees, gravestones, and a little shack where the men who work here take their coffee breaks. A wrought iron fence runs around it, except on one side where the iron posts run out and the chain link fence begins.

Between the lines, filling up the space like colour, there's grass, a wild assortment of trees hovering like green clouds, and, of course, freckling the entire area, gravestones. Gravestones of marble, limestone, and granite. Gravestones on four legs or lying flat, gravestones with straight backs or leaning forward as if they're looking for something once placed before them. Gravestones breaking like fingernails, others new and polished, adorned with wreaths, little silver angels and flowers.

And standing in front of one of these gravestones, often enough to appear a fixture, was the woman in the green coat. For a long time that's the way Gwendolyn, in her own mind, referred to her. If the lady had had a dog with her, then Gwen would have invented some other designation having to do with the dog's breed. The woman with the whippet or the woman with the black Newfoundland, for Gwen, if I remember correctly, viewed life in general through the filter of dogs, the way some people see it through rose-coloured glasses.

As a matter of fact, a year after acquiring a small German Shepherd whom she called Sheba, Gwen was already dividing the entire human race down the middle into dog people and non-dog people. The non-dog people who passed her every day in the graveyard, were going a long way to ruining her life.

At that time, before Gwen told me this story, her dog Yettie seemed to have Gwen's entire existence on a leash. Gwen controlled the dog, in the sense that she told Yettie to "sit" or "heel," but it was perfectly obvious that in all the ways that counted, Yettie had control of Gwen. And it wasn't that Yettie was unusually demanding. She wasn't. In fact, she behaved beautifully, rarely advancing six steps before looking back to see if Gwen was following. It was as if centuries ago, they'd exchanged blood and made vows.

Of course, they did exchange blood, as I imagine do most dog owners with their beloveds. Gwen and I lived in the same apartment building, and I'd see her several times a day as I was walking home from the corner store. On one of these occasions, Gwen appeared out of the "right eye" entrance of the graveyard, her pale face and the pace at which she usually walked, greatly accelerated. She was with Yettie, and I could tell, more from Yettie's body than from Gwen's, that something was bothering the both of them. The dog's head was lowered and instead of speeding up to smell something on the grass and then waiting for a moment for Gwen to catch up, Yettie slinked along, her nose hanging down like a black flag at the level of Gwen's mid-calf.

As I got closer, I noticed one of Yettie's "scoop bags" was wrapped tightly around Gwen's arm and after a few more steps, it became apparent that Gwen was bleeding ferociously from somewhere under the plastic bag, which seemed to me a pathetic attempt to contain the mess. She was crying, more from shock, she said, than from anything else. But as we continued to talk, I realized the source of the shock had less to do with the dog bite, than the fact that several people walking through the graveyard, had seen Yettie inflict the wound. These people were "regulars" in the sense that Gwen encountered them every day cutting through the graveyard in their business suits on the way to work.

That summer, Gwen was already on her way to becoming the black sheep of the graveyard, by refusing to observe any of the big white signs erected a year ago on the wrought iron fence. One sign demanded that dogs be kept on a leash, another said "Please Respect the Graves — Keep to the Roadways Unless Paying Your Respects." I think there was another sign saying that dog owners should pick up after their dogs. The sign about picking up dog poo was the only one Gwen observed.

The other two signs meant nothing. I'd heard her squabbling with various graveyard "regulars," or perhaps "squabbling" is inaccurate, since usually she and the "regular" seemed ready to slit each other's throats. Usually the arguments were about

Yettie roaming around the graveyard free as a squirrel. Since Yettie was as harmless as a squirrel, I can understand how Gwen felt she was fighting for a squirrel's freedom; if not the absurdity of keeping a squirrel on a leash.

Mind you, I must say this dog bore little resemblance to a squirrel. In fact, she looked like a wolf, as if just behind her eyes, you could pull back a set of invisible curtains and a wolf would present herself. She looked even more like a wolf in some ways than a wolf itself, as if "wolfness" had been distilled a stage past the quintessence of wolf and poured like amber liquid into her body. And this is what most of the "regulars" must have observed — liquid wolf amber not on a leash. The yelling would begin. Then Gwen, torn between disbelief and exasperation, would shout, "She *is* on a leash, SHE'S ON A VERBAL LEASH!"

Others objected to the fact that Gwen, instead of keeping to the roadways, wove herself like a small needle in and around the gravestones. Yettie used them as hurdles, jumping joyously over them, and in winter, skidding on those that lay flat, obscured by ice and snow. From my bedroom window, I could see a good part of the graveyard, and from my armchair I'd watch them playing games with black knuckled sticks.

Gwen devoted a good two hours each day to throwing sticks, and she'd turned this activity into an art form. She seemed able to locate the spirit in sticks, throwing them so they'd land and scuttle along like rabbits for about seven feet. Perhaps she knew what kind of stick made a good throw, or perhaps she just brought out the best in any stick.

Over the years, watching her first with Sheba (bless that poor dog's soul) and then with Yettie, I've become convinced that

Gwen's love for them drew her to a strange dark place, a movie theater where the outdoors became focused through their senses, acquiring a vibrancy much brighter and more circumscribed than normal, and she was never able to turn around, walk out, and see it exactly the same way again. Things such as wide open spaces without traffic, and trees kind enough to relinquish sticks to the Salvation Army of dog walkers became the key preoccupations of her life.

The afternoon I saw Gwen with the scoop bag wrapped around her forearm, she explained to me it was her fault. They had both lunged for the stick at the same time. Yettie wouldn't hurt Gwen intentionally, any more than Gwen would hurt her. When I think of the love between them, the word "transcendence" comes to mind, a word that in my day was much bandied about at dinner tables, but which seems to have gone out of fashion.

But where was I? I'm an elderly woman and sometimes lose my way. Gwen's behaviour in the graveyard wasn't a clear-cut case of disrespect, though perhaps I'm not judging her harshly enough. She was very good to me over the years, re-painting my walls when they needed it, running errands when my back hurt, and coming upstairs when she sensed that loneliness was throwing a dark shadow across the lawn of my life.

In any case, I'm not the only one who enjoyed her company. So did the gravediggers, although I suppose "gravediggers" is the wrong word nowadays. These men, once the ground had thawed, drove around in big machines with long-toothed shovels, and the rest of the time, tended to the grounds. Often too, they just stood like weathered pieces of board against their shack, smoking cigarettes and watching passers by. They were a feckless lot as, I imagine, are most men who work in groups, digging things up when the weather is pleasant. Gwen always stopped to chat with them, sometimes for a considerable amount of time.

The gravediggers had no objections to what others viewed as Gwen's disregard for the city ordinances, and for the dead and their sacred markers. They harboured few illusions about the graveyard, dealing with the bodies or remains as they did in the most material manner, as if they were worn out dollar bills that have passed through too many hands in their lives and are ready to be withdrawn from circulation.

They adjusted a stone when the wind or a gang of rebel youth had broken in during the night, and kicked one over. And they watched the ice nibble at the names and dates until they joked that the gravestones were made of cheese.

The only thing the gravediggers were really concerned about was vandalism. They realized somebody had paid a lot for these stones, and deserved to have them kept in good condition. They explained to Gwen that the increasing vandalism was the reason for the signs encouraging passersby to stick to the roadways. The sign ALL DOGS MUST BE KEPT ON A LEASH had been put up to discourage dogs from biting the ankles of people paying their respects, and to prevent dogs from running around in packs. They reassured Gwen that obviously her dog was happy and would bite no one on the leg, let alone run about the graveyard in a pack.

Ideas often present themselves to me in moon phases, so they appear on certain nights completely full, while at other times a negativity (loss of memory perhaps) gnaws them into quarter profiles, and I have to wait until they come around again, staring at me straight in the face. Looking back, the phrase "Yettie seemed to have Gwen's entire existence on a leash" sticks out on the page like a loose hem hanging down from a skirt. It needs fixing so that you might begin to realize what it is I mean.

In my younger days, I possessed an eagerness to learn, to travel around the world, to spend evenings in the company of people discussing politics, literature, music and painting. Some of these things I accomplished — enough for me to believe that now, sitting in my apartment with a good book, I am for the most part satiated. My removal from the world in which younger people buzz around amidst the flowers of opportunity, dreaming of honeys not yet tasted, seems to me a natural state of affairs for someone my age. The point I am trying to make is that Gwen, at the age of twenty-five, lived a life almost parallel to mine. It was as if she had parachuted across forty-odd years, wanting nothing more than the simplest pleasures — peace and quiet, fresh air and solitude, wanting nothing more than what she had, which I now think was less than I required myself, for she neither read nor listened to music. In the evenings, after taking Yettie for a long walk, she would place a log in the fireplace and just sit there, the only music in the room provided by the sound of Yettie chewing on a bone.

It occurred to me that she lived this way in order to harmonize her life, first with Sheba, and then in a more drastic way with Yettie. Yettie, Gwen said, abhorred noise; even the sound of the kitchen fan or a window closing would send her running from the room. And if Gwen tried to read something, Yettie would drop a ball between the pages in an effort to seduce Gwen into playing. Gwen couldn't say no to Yettie, since she considered it her duty not only to act as the Alpha Male in the relationship, but to fulfill the role of what in nature would be a litter mate.

Before Yettie, there was Sheba whom she had inherited from an earlier marriage. I don't know much about this marriage except that she came out of it with a bit of money, and the dog which had originally belonged to whoever she was married to. Apparently, they had a custody battle for the dog. Gwen lost the battle because, quite simply, Sheba had been bought by her original owner. But then, this owner got a contract in France and decided, after all this trouble, to leave the dog in Gwen's care.

Gwen once confided to me that she thought it unnatural that dogs should live with human beings, confined for most of their lives to apartment buildings, backyards, or houses. She believed that most dog owners were unwilling to make the compromises necessary for their animals to live like animals. She claimed they needed tons of fresh air, a walk every three hours, and someone to play with — anything else bordered on abuse. During her marriage, she was drawn into Sheba's needs, curtailing most of her activities, and even the time she spent with her husband.

Gwen also talked to her dog. Continually. Not just in the privacy of her own home, but outside as well. If the dog misbehaved, she grabbed it by the scruff of its neck, despite its size, lift it right off the ground, and establish eye contact, adjusting her head so that the animal's gaze couldn't escape. I asked her once if she thought Yettie understood 10% of what she was saying, and Gwen said sharply, "Dogs don't mind what they don't understand." Actually Gwen's animals understood quite a lot of what Gwen said — statements revolving around the words "food-bowl, ball, stick, puddle, snow, sidewalk, and grass," but her rather complex explanations? I doubt it.

When I first met Gwen, she worked at The Paradise Bakery, a small outlet on a dusty street in the North End of the city, renowned for their multi-grained bread. She went back and forth by bus, because she dreaded cars, and had never learned to drive. Which I now think is why she became so dependent on the graveyard. It was a beautiful place to walk through, full of trees. At first, she confused me. Just before my hip operation, coming downstairs slowly on my walker, I'd hear her call out to someone, "I'm off to Paradise!" And then eventually "Paradise is closing," until one afternoon I stopped her and asked what in the world she meant.

After Sheba died, Gwen was left with the life but not the dog she loved so much that she had allowed it to define the contours of her existence. She was like a woman living in a corrupt, uninhabitable world, who finds a squirrel-child in swaddling clothes on her doorstep, and decides to care for it, in the process coming to love this squirrel-creature more than life itself. Then the thing dies, and the woman is at such a loss she travels the world looking desperately for a similar specimen. Finding none, she returns home with two options: she can bring a child of her own into the world, or put her hunger aside, like a rich dessert she has tasted and, for the sake of her health, has resisted. Gwen wanted another shepherd desperately, but whereas her relationship with Sheba had evolved out of compassion, any new relationship would begin with her own neediness, and the process of acknowledging this unsavoury aspect of her character. In the end, she caved in and bought Yettie.

When Paradise closed, instead of looking for work elsewhere, Gwen stayed home making bread and pastries for customers who had complained bitterly when the bakery was going out of business. From what I gather, this enterprise was borne out of an overriding desire to be with Yettie at all times. "So Yettie won't get lonely," she told me, "Dogs have a pack mentality, and don't like to be left alone." She rarely went out with friends, and had no interest in any activity that Yettie couldn't share. It struck me as unnatural, and yet at the same time, our two solitudes, different as they were, became the common thread that ran between us. I stopped by her apartment several times a month to find her baking something, while Yettie sat cleaning out one of the mixing bowls.

In many ways, I will always associate Gwen with my hip operation because I met her shortly before I went into hospital. That day when I stopped her and asked what in God's name she meant by "Paradise is closing," she in turn asked me, "Why are you using a walker?" I responded by providing an avalanche of information, completely out of proportion to the actual question. To tell the truth, I was a nervous wreck, and her question was like a small hole that opened in the sky to let all my worries rain down and touch someone else. I never wanted to be like this, never thought I could be like this. By *this*, I mean one of those old women who snag young girls in hallways and with a simple question create a foundation on which to build an empire's worth of monologues.

And the girls, they stand there . . . their apartment keys held tight in their sticky palms, unable to get inside.

Except Gwen didn't seem to mind. I told her everything: that for a year I had terrible pains in my hip, but the doctors said it was nothing. That I had walked around on my shattered hip for a year until they did X-rays, and discovered that the whole right side of my hip had disintegrated, and I was actually walking around on nothing. Then they booked surgery, and I had to wait eight months for the operation, while I tried to get around on one hip. The surgery was the least of my worries. It was the recovery period when I would be sent home alone, incapable of even tying my shoelaces. The hospital had given me a handbook, entitled *You and Your Hip*, detailing the do's and don't's of the recovery period.

Do not bend your upper body forward more than a 90 degree angle to your hip.

Do not sit in chairs lower than knee height.

Do not sit on regular toilet seats.

My bed, they said, had to be elevated above knee height as well, but I hadn't the faintest idea where to get the materials to raise it, nor how I would raise it, should these materials appear miraculously on my front door mat. "Surely," they said to me, "you must have family . . . someone you can call on to help you." "Of course," I said brightly. Because I did have family — one made up of the multi-faceted characters I came across in novels, or the composers whose music I breathed while preparing a late night omelete. But none of them, unfortunately, was capable of raising my bed. And this is where Gwen came in. She offered to do it. Not only that, she volunteered to look around the second hand stores for an appropriate chair — something straight-backed and no lower than the height of my knees. Paradise, she informed me, would be closing in two weeks time, after which we'd have a month (before I went into hospital) to fix up my apartment.

And this is where the story really begins, if it could be said to begin anywhere at all. The afternoon Gwen raised my bed, she arrived with a stack of books, and several small saucers to place under each of the four legs. These surprised me because she had said she would build four wooden boxes. But books, she said, carrying a box full into my bedroom, would work even better. That Gwen chose to raise my bed with books may seem too symbolic somehow, but I assure you, dear Reader, it actually happened. Of course, she knew I loved books because the day she brought the straight-backed chair, she commented on the shelf of old, valuable books dominating my small living room.

Now I think of it, Gwen must have spent a great deal of time in the second-hand bookstore finding the right kind of books, by which I mean four piles of books with exactly the same dimensions, books big enough not to crumble under the weight of my bed. It would have been much easier to build four wooden boxes, but her method of raising my bed transcended the practical.

She refused to let me watch her unpack the books; she marched straight into the bedroom and closed the door behind her, yelling "It'll be done in a minute." I couldn't tell whether she thought I was hard of hearing or whether she imagined the walls to be thicker than they were. Or perhaps she enjoyed raising her voice. Even then, I'd heard her shouting in the graveyard. When she'd finished, she beckoned me into the bedroom.

"Well," she said, "what do you think?"

"It looks wonderful," I said, somewhat flummoxed by her enthusiasm.

It did look wonderful, in the sense that my bed had been effectively raised and, God knows, that was a load off my mind.

I made an effort to bend down and examine the books, and then remembered that my mobility was compromised.

"You might have positioned the books so I could read their spines," I said, "and tell which books I'll be recovering on!" Gwen had placed them with their spines facing inwards, rubbing shoulders with the dust bunnies under the bed.

"You'll have to wait until your hip is completely healed to find out what they are, and then you can keep them and read them," she said. "I just hope you don't have them. But, if you do, they weren't that expensive."

I realized then, this waiting game had been in her mind the whole time. This is the reason she chose books instead of boxes. It was a waiting game to distract from the other waiting game, for in my mind, I couldn't help but count the days until a sharp metallic blade would be shoved down into my thigh bone.

After she finished with the bed, we sat down at my kitchen table where I'd set out some large mugs, and a wild assortment of herbal teas, and looked at the *You and Your Hip* Patient Guide.

"Gwen, is it just my imagination or does that thing look like a dagger?" I said, pointing to the horrific picture of the ball and stem, and the cup to be placed in the socket (acetabulum) of my pelvic bone.

"No," Gwen replied, "it *does* look like a dagger."

I asked her then if she thought they'd be taking a drill to my femur bone, and she said she supposed so, but didn't know for sure. And finally the day came when I hobbled to the hospital (only a block away) for my hip replacement, the idea of the dagger firmly implanted in my mind, although Gwen had advised me not to think about the whole thing in terms of a dagger.

"Well, how should I think about it?" I demanded. "In terms of a flower?"

She looked away, as it is easier to replace a hip than replace an image by which your entire mind is held hostage. That morning was a drizzle of concrete and sky. In the graveyard two of the diggers pulled back the heavy iron gates. Oh, I thought to myself, if I could just wake up beside a vase of daggers and a flower (what kind would it be?) linking my bones. If only it were possible to find a kind that resembles a dagger, but what in God's name would it be? What likenesses buzz around the hive of what a dagger is?

The next thing I knew, time had passed. I woke up in a drug-induced state. I was nauseous and my thigh and knee were engaged in an impossible tug of war. The fact is that a portion of one's life can be removed as easily as a tissue from one of those pop-out Kleenex boxes. The boxes in hospital were small and white and somewhat flattened. What a ridiculous thing to remember! The memory is a poorly designed thing. It is democratic to a fault, recalling at the most inopportune times all the garbage swept into the eye's dustbin. It wouldn't surprise me if I died remembering nothing more significant than the white Kleenex boxes I encountered in hospital. Or the religious nut-bar in Bed Three. Or the paper cone cups my eyes grazed over while wandering in the direction of the sink.

Yes, there were many nights like that. The light from the hallway seared through the room. The nut-bar in Bed Three kept us all awake with his morose, nonsensical prophesies. By "all of us" I mean myself, the gentleman in Bed Two and the nut-bar as well, of course, because I'm convinced that parts of his own body must have been rebelling against the tyranny of sleeplessness. Every so often, the gentleman in Bed Two would groan, then pipe up, "Ahh, come on now, will you cut that out!" And eventually, "Oh for Christ's sake, shut up, will you?"

This gentleman, recovering from foot surgery (the eleventh surgery on the same foot) was separated from the nut-bar by a sole curtain, while I lay across from Bed Two in a little alcove.

In truth, I possessed the most favourable spot in the room. There was a window to my right so that on bright days my bed sheets virtually dazzled. To my left, there was the sink with the paper cone cups. And beyond the sink was the door through which people constantly poked their heads — trying to locate whomever they were trying to locate (grandmother? uncle? sister?) in the labyrinth of hospital wings — and then just as quickly withdrawing them.

But a word about the prophet. He attributed a numerical value to every letter in the alphabet and spent his time adding up what he felt were significant words, names, and events. These he interpreted according to a book he owned called *Numbers In Scripture*. He come to the conclusion that the world would end on December the twelfth. Nearly every half hour he made this declaration, and followed it with evidence consisting of biblical passages, numerical equations, and a series of contingent conclusions.

When I woke up, I asked the nurse whether it was my first day in hospital. The prophet, before the nurse could respond, said, "Number One equals the light which cannot be divided and the sovereignty of God." The nurse said, "Jack, hush, there are people trying to sleep." I can't recall much of Day One or Day Two. The painkiller blanked me out for hours until someone woke me. Once the surgeon informed me that he'd spent most of the operation peeling away pieces of bone like onion. I told him about the tug-of-war between my knee and my hip, and he offered the serene explanation that perhaps my muscles had shortened in the prolonged period I'd walked around basically hip-less.

Unlike any regular visitor I've ever encountered, Gwen spent four hours at a time paying her respects. During her first visit I said, "I'm tired now, I fear I may fall asleep."

"That's okay," she said, "go ahead and sleep, I'll just sit here."

And so I fell asleep, sometimes to wake up and find her beside me. Other times, I'd hear her talking to the prophet. Originally, she'd disappeared behind the curtain saying, "sshhh, people are trying to sleep." Instead of coming right back out, she stayed there for God knows how long, talking to him. I could hear the conversation — one of his numerical declarations, then Gwen asking him something, his frank delight in having been asked, and then his responding in great detail, showing her this, showing her that.

She did other things as well, even while I was awake. She'd wander into the hallway and take her blood pressure. Several times a day, she'd go and look for a discarded newspaper with a blank crossword puzzle. Finding one, from what I could gather was quite a feat. While a newspaper itself was easy to find finding one with a blank crossword was a completely different story. Every patient, it seemed, had a penchant for crosswords. I, myself, have never bothered with newspapers, but I do enjoy a good crossword. Nevertheless, I wasn't about to pay the price of a newspaper to do a single crossword. And this is how the crossword-hunt began.

What else did she do to amuse herself? Once, she got into a wheelchair and wheeled herself outside to have a cigarette — since the hospitals by this time were all non-smoking.

"Gwen," I said, as she borrowed a cigarette from the gentleman with the bad foot, "I didn't know you smoked!"

"I don't," she said, "I just feel like being a disabled smoker."

When she returned in her wheelchair, she told me that everyone had been exceptionally kind to her, opening doors… and the smokers themselves, of course, rushing up to light her cigarette. Upon hearing this, the gentleman asked Gwen whether she would wheel him down so that he could have a smoke. An expression of alarm scooted across her face.

"What if the same people are outside?" she said. "What will they think, especially after everyone took pity on me?"

"How do you know they took pity on you?" the gentleman said.

"Don't worry, Gwen!" the prophet shouted from behind his curtain. "The world's gonna end anyway. On December the twelfth."

"Will you stop that nonsense!" the gentleman groaned, "I think we've had enough of that!"

"I could just tell," Gwen said.

Then a nurse walked in to attend to the prophet, Gwen agreed to take the gentleman out for a cigarette while I, in turn, shut my eyes and attempted to will the painful throbbing out of my thigh.

"You don't have to worry about doing your Christmas shopping this year," I heard from behind the curtain . . .

Cello player, ESL teacher, and writer EMILY GIVNER was born in Regina, Saskatchewan. She died July 5th, 2004 in Halifax, Nova Scotia, of an allergic reaction, aged 38. From birth Emily's life had been complicated and restricted by asthma and allergy problems though she refused to let her aliments interfere with her life of travel, music and writing. On her death she left a considerable amount of writing — files of letters home recording her experiences in different countries, essays on the writing process and a substantial collection of unpublished stories and novellas.